FINDING HOME

CAROLYNE AARSEN

Misty Ridge Publishing

Finding Home was previously released as Catching Her Heart.

❀ Created with Vellum

CHAPTER 1

*I*t wasn't supposed to happen this soon. She wasn't supposed to see him yet. She wasn't ready.

Naomi ran her suddenly damp palms over her apron. She grabbed the tray of fresh-baked brownies and slipped them into the display case of Mug Shots, the café she worked at part-time. Then she straightened and looked directly into the eyes of Jess Schroder and the part of her past she spent years trying to keep buried.

Good-looking as ever, she thought, her heart doing the same silly flip it always did whenever she saw him all those years ago. Time had filled out his broad shoulders, narrowed his waist, lent interesting shadows and hollows to his handsome features. He still wore his hair a little long and it still waved over his forehead and into his eyes, but it had darkened from the blond it used to be to a light brown. His square jaw was shadowed by stubble, narrow nose, chiseled features and dark eyes that seemed to drill into her very soul.

"What can I get you?" she asked, pleased that her voice could sound so casual.

He shot her a frown, as if surprised that she didn't swoon at his feet. Like she almost did every day that summer she tutored him.

That summer they dated.

"Hey, Naomi," he said quietly, slipping his hand in the back pocket of his blue jeans. "I heard you were back in town."

His deep voice tugged at memories she thought had been lost in the onslaught of what had happened since that summer they spent together ten years ago.

Please, Lord, help me through this. Help me to stay focused on You.

Her prayer was a cry from a wounded heart still struggling after her fiancé's death. From the move back from a place she had lived for the past ten years. Moving from Halifax had been difficult but after Billy's death, she needed to come back to her family. Especially now that all her cousins were settled back in Rockyview.

Nursing Billy the past few months of his life had been wrenching, difficult but she never once regretted the time she had spent with him.

She knew when she came back to Rockyview she would be seeing Jess again. She thought she had prepared herself for it.

But from the way her heart hammered in her chest, guess not.

She drew in another long breath, then another and thankfully, she felt her equilibrium return.

"I got back a few weeks ago," she said, thankful that her feelings didn't seep into her voice.

Jess's expression grew suddenly serious. "I heard about Billy. I was sorry to hear about his death."

Before she could acknowledge his sympathy, the door of the café opened again and an unfamiliar young girl, obviously pregnant, came inside and waddled over to Jess's side. "So, Jess, you buying me lunch?" she asked. The girl eased out a sigh as she pushed her black hair away from her face.

Naomi glanced from Jess to the girl who didn't look a day

over sixteen and then at her protruding stomach. Her emotions spun again as she tried to reconcile the girl's age with the man standing in front of her.

The man who had once held her heart.

"Naomi, this is Brittany. My stepsister," Jess said so hastily he almost stuttered on the last words. "My mother married her father five years ago."

Why did that piece of information make her feel relieved? Because she didn't want to think that poorly of a man she had once cared for so deeply?

She mentally clung on to a memory of Billy to remind her that she should be thinking of him, not reliving old romances. Billy had been such a good, caring man. One of the best things that happened to her. She often regretted that she couldn't return the love he gave her. At the same time, she was so thankful he understood. Though he had told her she didn't have to stay, she made the choice to be by his side to the end. To be faithful to him with her presence and support him to the end.

"Brittany, this is Naomi," Jess was saying, turning to the young girl, continuing the introduction. "Naomi and I...we used...used to go to school together."

Brittany frowned. "You look familiar. Do I know you?"

Naomi shook her head. "I doubt it. I don't think we've met." She didn't even know Jess had a stepsister.

"Brittany and my mother, *our* mother," Jess corrected, "moved here from Victoria and they're staying with me for a while."

"Staying until I pop," the girl said, shifting her weight, wavering. Her eyes were ringed with black, but the foundation on her face couldn't hide the shadows under her eyes and the general pallor of her complexion. A drop of perspiration trickled down the side of her face, leaving a track in her makeup. "My dad died a couple of months ago and now Sheila doesn't know what to do with me, and I got nowhere else to go."

The belligerent tone in her voice hid a deeper hurt that called to Naomi. Her mother didn't always know what to do with Naomi and her sisters either. Thankfully they had Nana and Papa Bond and their cousins, Garret and Tanner, and the ranch. She and her sisters spent many weekends and summers there as a family.

Seemed like Brittany had no one but Jess.

"I'm so sorry to hear that," Naomi said quietly.

Brittany shot her a puzzled glance, as if surprised by her pity. Then she waved her hand, as if dismissing it. "I need to eat," she moaned. "I'm starving and so thirsty I could drink a gallon of pop."

Jess gave her a tight smile, then pulled his wallet out of his back pocket. He glanced up at the board running along the top of the wall on which Naomi had painstakingly written the menu for the day in colored chalk. The flowers and little flourishes she had added seemed cute at the time and had been heartily endorsed by Kerry, the owner, but as Jess raised one perfectly arched eyebrow they seemed childish and foolish.

"I'm guessing you wrote that?" he said, chucking his chin toward the board. "I recognize the doodles." He said that with a quick smile that was supposed to be a shared joke.

Naomi nodded, a flush working its way up the back of her neck. Too well she remembered drawing the same flourishes and flowers in his workbook while she coached him through mathematic and chemistry equations. He teased her then, too, as they lay on their stomachs in the grassy mountain meadow overlooking Rockyview.

"Jess, please, I'm dying of thirst and hunger here," Brittany moaned. "Just get me something. Anything."

"Okay. I guess we'll start with a bottle of water for Brittany here," Jess said. "And I'll have—"

"Jess," Brittany called out. "Help me..." Her voice faltered and the teenager tilted, clutched Jess's arm, then slumped to the floor.

"Brittany, what's wrong? Brit?" Jess dropped to the floor beside her, his voice holding an edge of panic.

Naomi ran around the counter. A collective gasp went up in the café as people at the nearest table got up, as well. Naomi slipped her arm around Brittany's shoulders to support her. Brittany's eyes rolled in her sockets, her breathing erratic. "Brittany, talk to me," Naomi urged, hoping, praying the girl stayed conscious. "What's wrong? Is it the baby?"

"I feel funny. I...I can't see." She blinked and caught Naomi's hand in a crushing grip. "Help me. I'm scared."

"Call 9-1-1," Naomi called out as she laid her finger on the girl's neck to check her pulse, bending over to listen to her breathing, trying to block out the startled murmurs of the other customers in the café.

Then she caught what smelled like old apples on Brittany's breath. Her mind flashed back to Brittany begging for something to drink, saying how hungry she was and her nurse's aide training came back.

Ketoacidosis.

"What's wrong?" Jess asked as he pulled out his cell phone, panic in his voice. "Do you know what's wrong with her?"

"I think I do. Help me carry her," Naomi said. "It will be faster for us to bring her to the hospital ourselves. It's only a couple of blocks away." She called out for Kerry telling her she had to leave.

Jess bent over, fitted his arms under Brittany's legs and shoulders and in one easy motion, stood. But the girl still clung to Naomi's hand.

Someone had run ahead and was opening the door to the patio as Jess rushed through, surprisingly quick considering his burden.

"My keys are in my shirt pocket," Jess grunted as they got to his truck.

Naomi fished them out and handed them to another bystander who unlocked the doors. Naomi managed to pry her hand loose from Brittany's grip, but the girl gasped, then pleaded, terror lacing her voice. "No. Please. Don't go."

"Come with me," Jess said as he lay Brittany in the backseat of the truck's cab.

Naomi didn't think. She got into the back with Brittany and held the girl's head on her lap. Seconds later they squealed out of the parking lot and headed toward the hospital.

Brittany found Naomi's hand again and clung tightly.

"You'll be okay," Naomi assured her, stroking her hair away from her damp face. "You'll be okay once we get to the hospital."

Then she began praying.

"Your sister has acute hyperglycemia, probably brought on by her pregnancy. It's why she collapsed." Dr. Brouwer delivered this news in a quiet voice as he stood on the other side of Brittany's bed beside Naomi. His white lab coat was a sharp contrast to his short dark hair and the stubble shading a strong jaw. Jess had never met him before and only knew that Ben Brouwer was an experienced ER doctor and was engaged to Naomi's sister, Shannon.

But his quiet presence and calm voice assured Jess his step-sister was in good hands.

Jess could only nod, his eyes still on Brittany's quiet form, lying on the bed between them. Her dark hair lay fanned out on the pillow and her features hung slack. A tube ran out of one arm to an IV. Other lines snaked away from her body hooked up to a monitor beeping above the bed in the emergency room. He didn't know what it meant, but he guessed the regular wave pattern meant Brittany's heart was working properly.

His own heart was still recuperating from the sudden shock. Seeing Brittany keel over like that had sucked all the air out of his lungs.

He looked over at Naomi who had been so calm through the whole thing, staying with them both, holding Brittany's hand and reassuring the girl in her soft, modulated voice. She was looking down at Brittany now, her hand on his stepsister's head, her eyes hooded by her lowered lashes.

He wished he could read her expression.

He wished their first meeting in ten years hadn't happened under such dramatic circumstances.

Ever since he heard Naomi Deacon was back in Rockyview, he tried to avoid seeing her. It had been difficult. Rockyview wasn't that big. He'd had to get his coffee elsewhere once he found out she was working at Mug Shots. One time he saw Shannon and her coming out of Evangeline's bookstore and he had to duck into the hardware store to avoid her. It hadn't turned out great because he forgot that Dietrich Bogal didn't own the hardware store anymore. Naomi's soon-to-be-brother-in-law, Dan, had bought it. So he ended up ducking into the pots and pans aisle to avoid him.

Now, with Naomi standing across the bed from him, he was disappointed that even after all this time, memories of that day she left him still resurrected a sharp ache.

"So what does that mean?" Jess asked, dragging his attention back to Dr. Brouwer.

"It means her pregnancy is putting an extra strain on her pancreas and it isn't manufacturing enough insulin, which your body needs to access the glucose in your blood. The glucose builds up and the body starts to shut down because it doesn't have the fuel it needs to function."

As Dr. Brouwer talked about insulin and diet and blood

sugar levels, all Jess could do was nod, his head was spinning as he struggled to absorb all the information coming at him. He didn't know how to take care of a normal sixteen-year-old girl, let alone one who was pregnant and now, apparently, diabetic.

Not for the first time he felt a surge of frustration with his situation. His mother had unexpectedly dropped into his life, Brittany in tow, a couple of days ago. His mother was grieving the death of her second husband, she said, and wanted to be back in Rockyview. Then, this morning, she left, saying she needed to be alone for a few days. Could Jess watch Brittany? His mother had assured him she'd be back soon.

Jess wasn't thrilled with the arrangement. Having a young girl staying with him, a bachelor, didn't look good. So this morning he moved into his new, unfinished house, leaving Brittany alone in the old house. But what was he supposed to do now that she was sick?

"...and because she is also pre-eclampsia, we need to put her on bed rest."

"Say what?" The doctor's last words snagged his attention. "Bedrest? What's that about?"

"I'm concerned about her blood pressure." Dr. Brouwer turned to Naomi, his dark eyes holding a surprising concern. "Do you mind staying with her a moment?" he asked. "I'd like to talk to Jess."

"I'll be fine, Ben," she said. The sight of her easy smile created an ache deep in Jess's chest. Since they arrived at the hospital, Naomi hadn't spoken to him or made eye contact, creating a palpable unease and a measure of frustration for him. He wondered why she still mattered to him when he knew he mattered so little to her.

Dr. Brouwer motioned to him, walking out of the cubicle of the emergency room. Jess blindly followed, his mind shifting to what he needed to process.

Bed rest. Pregnancy-related diabetes. Pre-eclampsia.

The words swirled around his head like crows, waiting to pounce on him with their hard reality.

Dr. Brouwer stopped at the desk where a nurse was busy typing up some notes into a computer, then turned to Jess. "I don't know what your situation is, but taking care of Brittany will be a full-time job. Is her mother in the picture?"

Jess just stared at him, his frustration with his mother reaching an all-time high. "She's gone right now. I have to call her to tell her what happened."

Dr. Brouwer frowned, his arms folded across his chest, as if trying to puzzle out the relationship. "She's your sister, isn't she?"

"Step-sister of sorts. After my parents divorced, my mother remarried a man who already had Brittany. She's not related to me or my mother." He shoved his hand through his hair, then dropped his hands on his hips holding Dr. Brouwer's curious gaze. He wasn't about to spill out the mess of his and his mother's life right now. "Right now she's my responsibility, so what should I do?"

"I would recommend hiring a personal nurse in the interim. She, or he, doesn't need to be a registered nurse, but they do need some sort of nursing experience or training. You might want them at your house as much as possible."

"So where do I find someone like that?"

Dr. Brouwer pulled at his lower lip, as if thinking. "Naomi is a trained Licensed Practical Nurse. She spent the past year taking care of her fiancé who was dying from cancer. Before that she did some work as an LPN. And your sister seems to have formed an attachment to her."

Jess shook his head. He had barely gotten used to the idea that Naomi was back. To have her right under his nose for who knows how long—

"I'll see who else I can find," he said, realizing he was being borderline rude ignoring Dr. Brouwer's suggestions. "I've got a couple of days."

"At best. Once Brittany is stable, we can't keep her in the hospital very long. In addition, someone needs to come with her to learn alongside her before she's discharged."

Jess frowned again. "Learn what?"

"Diabetes, especially pregnancy-related diabetes, requires a learning curve with diet, lifestyle change, blood test regimen and insulin injection. Normally we do the teaching only to the patient, but Brittany is quite young yet so it would be best if you, or your mother, could come in every day and learn the protocol, as well."

Jess wasn't prone to headaches, but the tightness in his forehead told him that one was on its way. "So when does this start?"

"Monday afternoon."

Which was when the plumber was coming. Jess had been waiting for a month for this guy to come. If he begged off now it would be months before he could get him back again.

"If you hired Naomi, you wouldn't need to go through the training," Dr. Brouwer continued. "She could take care of Brittany as soon as she is stable."

He made it sound as if there would be no problem with Jess having Naomi so close every day. Jess wondered if his fiancée Shannon or her sister Hailey or even Naomi had filled Dr. Brouwer in on the details of his and Naomi's previous relationship.

Doubtful. Jess was fairly sure that Naomi had glossed over those months they spent together when Naomi tutored him and when he, like a fool, had fallen in love. Had thought that Naomi felt the same. But when Billy, Naomi's ex-boyfriend, came back from his mission trip in Belize, Naomi ran back to him so fast, her running shoes almost left skid marks on Jess's floor.

"I'll hire someone, but I prefer it not be Naomi."

Dr. Brouwer only nodded, then looked past him, and by the all-too-familiar tingle at the back of his neck he knew Naomi stood behind him.

He turned, catching a look of puzzled hurt, which was quickly replaced by a forced smile and a light laugh.

"Hire me for what?" she asked, her voice even. As if that moment of weakness had never happened.

"I was trying to persuade Jess to hire you as a personal nurse for his sister," Dr. Brouwer said.

"Probably not a good idea," she said quietly, then walked past them both, her ponytail bobbing behind her.

Dr. Brouwer glanced from Naomi to Jess, his frown clearly showing his puzzlement.

Jess turned back to Dr. Brouwer. "So what are my other options?"

Dr. Brouwer lifted one shoulder in a shrug. "I can ask around and see if one of the part-time nurses here would be willing to work a few extra days."

"Let me know what you find out."

Dr. Brouwer nodded and Jess walked back to his stepsister's bed, the weight of her care dragging at him with hard, heavy hands.

Even if his mother did come back, he was fairly sure she wouldn't be much help for Brittany.

He stood beside her, looking down at this girl who he barely knew. She looked so lost and alone, his heart went out to her. His mother had been an absent mother to him for much of his life, too.

As for his father?

Jess curled his fists at the memory of a man who had dominated his life in so many ways. He still bore the scars of his father's anger on his body and his soul. As a result hatred for his father ran deep and had become ingrained in his heart. Naomi had talked about forgiveness, but he hadn't been able to follow through on it.

Naomi.

His heart clenched at the thought of her. He'd had enough hurt in his life. He certainly wasn't putting himself in the path of more by hiring Naomi Deacon.

Not if he could help it.

CHAPTER 2

"*Y*ou made the right decision," Shannon said in her best big-sister voice. "Working for Jess right now is not a good idea."

Naomi took a sip of her coffee as she glanced around the gathering at Nana Bond's house. It was the fourth Sunday of the month and on those Sundays it was decreed that everyone come to Nana's place after church for Sunday dinner.

"You're still grieving. It's too soon after Billy's death. Besides, I know how upset you were after Jess broke up with you that summer."

"That was ten years ago," Naomi said, as much to remind herself as her sister. "And I was with Billy for all of the time after that."

Besides, Jess didn't even want to hire me. In fact, he preferred anyone else but me.

"I also know how crazy you were about Jess," Shannon continued, determined to drag out a past Naomi was trying to put behind her. "And whenever I saw you with him you seemed —" She stopped there, pulling the corner of her lip in as if trying to stop herself from saying anything else.

Leave it, a tiny voice warned her. Just leave it be. But Naomi's curiosity got the better of her. Shannon and Hailey had expended a lot of energy warning her against getting romantically involved with Jess Schroder, warning her all those years ago that he wasn't her type. He would be bad for her. He was a player who would dump her and move on.

If only they knew.

"I seemed what?" Naomi prompted.

"Doesn't matter," Shannon said, brushing her question aside.

"No, tell me." Like an itch she couldn't scratch, she couldn't let her sister's unfinished comment simply fade away.

Shannon looked down at her hands, fiddling with her engagement ring, then sent her sister a quick look, easing out a reluctant sigh. "You seemed more alive with Jess than you ever did with Billy. Happier."

Naomi acknowledged her sister's comment, her mind slipping back to Jess as if testing what his memory would do to her. Thinking of his unexpected appearance at Mug Shots on Friday could still create that nervous flutter she'd experienced every time she'd seen him strolling down the halls of Rockyview High School. Jess Schroder was the kind of guy who turned heads and broke hearts. His good looks and wealthy parents were a combination guaranteed to get him almost any girl he wanted.

Including Naomi.

"That was before he dumped me. Before he let me hang. Before everything." Too late, she realized what her words sounded like and how they could be construed. The puzzled frown her sister sent her underlined that.

"What do you mean, 'everything'?"

Naomi felt the old secret rise up, like a living thing, but she pushed it back.

Then, thankfully, the conversation was truncated by the tinkling of a spoon against a cup.

With relief, Naomi turned to her cousin Tanner, who stood

in the middle of the living room, his arm around Sabine, his stepdaughter, Olivia, Sabine's daughter, standing beside her.

His dark hair waved away from a face lit up with a happiness that could only be described as euphoric. Sabine had one arm around his waist, her other hand rested on his chest in a solicitous gesture as her smoky-gray eyes looked up at him.

Naomi couldn't stop a smile at the sight. She had missed Tanner and Sabine's wedding, but had been thrilled for her cousin. After the death of his wife and stepdaughter almost four years ago, the family wondered if Tanner would ever return to the ranch or Rockyview. He did, then met Sabine and his life had fallen into pleasant places.

"I have an announcement to make," he said glancing down at Sabine and dropping a kiss on the top of her head. His happy gaze went first to his twin brother, Garret, who sat on the couch, his fiancée, Larissa, at his side, then to Shannon and Ben, then Hailey and her fiancé, Dan, and finally, resting on Naomi. A fleeting expression of sorrow for her tracked his features and then was replaced by another smile as Tanner turned to Nana Bond holding court in her easy chair. "In about six months this family will get bigger by one small baby."

Silence followed his announcement and then pandemonium broke out. Hailey squealed, jumped up from the couch and grabbed Tanner in a bear hug. Then Shannon got up and went to hug Sabine.

As for Nana Bond, she stayed in her chair, her hand over her mouth as if trying to absorb this wonderful information. Then she, too, was standing, joining Dan, Ben, Larissa, and Garret in congratulating the happy couple.

Naomi held back for a moment, disappointed at the hot tears gathering at the back of her throat. Tears of joy, she told herself as she swallowed them down. A little baby in the family. A great-grandchild for Nana Bond.

She blinked the moisture from her eyes, then moved toward

her cousin to congratulate him, his wife, Sabine, and their daughter, Olivia, in their happy news.

As she hugged Sabine, then Tanner, her thoughts moved to Brittany and her pregnancy. A single mother with no man at her side. Her heart ached for the young girl so alone.

"Isn't it wonderful news?" Nana was saying to Naomi, drawing her into the happy circle.

"It is," Naomi said. "I'm so happy for them."

Nana patted her on the arm. "I know coming back has been hard for you, but I'm so glad you're here. I feel like my family is complete."

Naomi gave her a quick smile, then dropped a kiss on her cheek. "I'm glad to be back, too. After all, I promised I would."

"And you're still looking for another job I hear?"

"Yes. There's a part-time job coming up at the hospital in less than a month. If I keep working at Mug Shots and take that job as well I'll get by."

Nana smiled and gave her a gentle hug. "Sounds like a good practical plan from a good, practical girl."

That's me, Naomi thought with a touch of asperity. *The good girl. The practical girl.*

If only they knew.

She thought back to Brittany again and promised herself she would stay at Nana's as long as was polite, then go visit her and see how she was doing.

An hour later Naomi stood outside the door of Brittany's hospital room, listening before going in. She didn't want to run into Jess. But it sounded like no one was visiting, so she stepped inside.

Brittany sat upright in her bed, staring straight ahead, the desolation on her face pulling at Naomi's heart.

"Hey, girl," she said. "You look a lot better than you did the last time I saw you."

Brittany's eyes lit up and Naomi knew she had done the right thing by coming. "I'm so glad to see you."

"How are you feeling?"

"Like I'm packing around a beach ball full of sand," Brittany said, her hands resting on her stomach as if protecting her unborn child.

Naomi laughed, but behind it she felt an echo of an old sadness and shame that the sight of this young, pregnant woman resurrected.

She whisked the memories aside, focusing on the present. "I was talking to Dr. Ben at my nana's place," she said, smoothing out a wrinkle in the sheets. "I understand you're being released this week. Is your mom coming to help?"

Brittany quickly averted her head, but before she did, Naomi saw her eyes glistening. "Sheila said she can't right now. She says she's got too much going on in her own life." Brittany reached up to push her hair away from her face. "Said she was still grieving my dad's death."

But so would Brittany, Naomi thought. Even though Sheila was grieving the loss of a husband, Brittany was grieving the loss of a father.

Naomi frowned at the selfishness of this woman and, at the same time, feeling some kinship with Brittany. Her own mother, Noelle Deacon, had moved back to Rockyview after her divorce and had, for the most part, left the care of her daughters to her parents. Thankfully, Nana and Papa had filled the void in Naomi's and her sister's lives and had given them a home on their ranch. But Naomi still had wished her mother had been more involved in their lives.

"I'm sure she's still sad but she'll come back to help you out."

"Why should she?" Brittany sniffed, still looking away as if ashamed of her weakness. "She's not even my real mother."

Naomi knew that.

Ten years ago Sheila had still been married to Jess's father. In fact, that summer that Jess and Naomi had been together, Jess's parents had been away in Barbados to ostensibly repair a marriage that had been faltering for years, according to Jess. Jess had been left behind with a housekeeper and a tutor to get him ready for his college entrance exams.

That tutor had been Naomi, and that summer the two of them had been, for the most part, on their own.

The summer Naomi had fallen in love with Jess.

Focus, Naomi. She turned back to the girl in the bed in front of her. "So did Jess manage to find someone to come and take care of you?" She was asking out of curiosity more than anything, she reminded herself. Curiosity and a concern for this young girl who seemed so alone.

Brittany shook her head. "No, and he's getting kind of grumpy about it." Then Brittany reached out and caught Naomi by the hand, gripping it as if holding on to a lifeline. "You're kind of like a nurse. Can you do it?"

Naomi squeezed the girl's hand back, trying to give her some kind of assurance.

"Please," Brittany pleaded, squeezing even tighter. "I don't know what I'm supposed to do. The nurses keep talking about food and diet and needles and blood tests and blood pressure and danger to the baby, and I'm scared and I know Jess doesn't have a clue."

Naomi felt her resolve faltering as she caught Brittany's fearful gaze. She wanted to help the girl, she really did. But helping her would mean being around Jess all day. She knew he was working on his house, which was only a couple of hundred feet away from the old house where Brittany was staying. Much too close.

Naomi had spent the past number of years supporting Billy in his work, then taking care of him when he got sick. He had dominated her life and she had let it happen. Getting close to Jess meant getting pulled into another vortex of emotions and memories. Memories and emotions she thought she had left behind, but were easily resurrected when she saw him again. She needed to figure out what she wanted to do, where she wanted to go with her life. Being around Jess would be too much of a distraction.

"Please, can you help me?" Brittany repeated, tears welling up in her eyes. "My mom isn't coming and I don't have anyone else."

Naomi's resolve wavered at the sight of the young girl's obvious anguish. Was she being selfish turning down Brittany's request because she wanted to guard her heart?

Please, Lord, tell me what to do?

Then she thought of Billy and how he'd taken her back even after she'd told him everything. She thought he would condemn her but instead, he'd folded her in his arms, drew her close and told her they would get through this.

Billy had so easily forgiven her and had been so willing to take her in. Taking care of Brittany could be a way for her to atone for what had happened all those years ago.

"If that's what you want, I'll do this for you," Naomi said, wrapping her hands around Brittany's. "I'll come and take care of you."

"Brittany needs you now." Jess clutched his cell phone, his frustration with his situation warring with his sympathy for his mother's sorrow. "Can't you come sooner?"

He was sitting in his truck, parked in front of the hospital. He'd missed church this morning because he needed to get things ready for the plumber tomorrow. Tomorrow he had to figure out how to be here to learn more about Brittany's care and work on his house.

"I am not in a good place," his mother said in a plaintive

voice. "I just need some time alone. I talked to Dr. Brouwer and he said he advised you to hire a personal nurse. Why don't you do that? If she stayed overnight you wouldn't have to worry about how things look, though I'm surprised you're so concerned."

Her tone implied that Jess never used to care about propriety. She used to be right. But he wasn't the wild and crazy young man he once was.

"I know you're still grieving, but so is Brittany."

His mother heaved out a sigh. "I'm sorry, but I'm no support for that poor girl."

Jess kneaded the back of his neck, feeling like he was being pushed into a corner he couldn't retreat from. He'd been able to go to the hospital yesterday and in the couple of hours he spent with the nurses, he knew he wasn't the right person to do this.

Unfortunately he'd also spent the rest of the day trying to find someone able and willing to be at his house when Brittany would be discharged.

So far his only option was Naomi.

Could he have Naomi around all the time, though? He had been so convinced he'd gotten over her, but even those few moments in the hospital had shown him how foolish that was.

But what choice did he have? Right now he had Brittany to think about, and the poor girl needed someone more capable than him to help her.

Please, Lord, he prayed, *I don't see a way out. Please send someone to do this job.*

He finished his conversation with his mother, got out of the truck and walked toward the hospital. He glanced up at the mountains surrounding the valley. Snow still clung to the topmost peaks. Behind him, Misty Ridge was clear of snow and the summer work was done. In a couple of weeks they would be closing down the chair lift used by the mountain bikers and hikers who would take the lift up, and bike or walk down the mountain. This winter he'd sold his cat-skiing operation and had hired someone else to manage the summer part of the ski hill. Which meant he could now work on the house he'd been trying to finish for the past four years and hopefully move in before the snow came and the winter season started up.

Would that even happen now that he had Brittany to take care of?

Jess shook his head, dropped his keys in his shirt pocket and trudged up the walk to the hospital. Something would come up. He just felt it.

He walked down the hallway to the room, then stopped when he heard Brittany talking.

"I'll come and take care of you."

Jess stood outside the door of the hospital room, Naomi's words ringing in the quiet following her announcement. What? What was she saying?

No, this couldn't happen.

Then Brittany squealed with happiness. "That's awesome. I'm so glad."

He thought of how his stepsister had clung to Naomi's hand and he sighed. He had just prayed for someone to come and do the job, hadn't he?

At the same time his doubts were eased away and he allowed himself some relief that Brittany's care was taken care of. But could he stand to see Naomi every day and keep his own emotions in check?

Then he squared his shoulders and pushed aside his foolish reaction. He and Naomi were adults. Sure they had dated at one time. Been close. No reason they couldn't move past that. Ten years was a long time ago. A decade.

He took a deep breath, then strolled into the room, the picture of casual.

Naomi stood by Brittany's bed, looking down, her long hair hanging loose and framing her face just the way Jess always liked it. The sweater she wore was the gold of the trees in the fall and set off her reddish-brown hair and hazel eyes. As she reached out and took Brittany's hand, Naomi's gentle smile transformed her features and brought out memories from the back of his mind. Naomi laughing and screaming as the tire tube they floated on plunged over the rapids. Naomi lying back on a picnic blanket in a quiet cove by the river, the hot summer sun drying them off, her face tipped to the sky, the same smile on her face as she declared the day to be like a perfect jewel, bright and shiny and precious.

Jess gripped his hands into fists, banishing the memories, replacing them with the sight of her with Billy a few months later. Perfect Billy who was going to be a minister. Billy who would never have taken advantage of her the way he had.

Then Brittany turned her head and saw Jess.

"Hey, Jess. Guess what? Naomi is going to take care of me." Brittany's exuberant grin and the joy bubbling out from her balanced out his own uncertainty about hiring Naomi. "You're off the hook now."

"Awesome," he said with forced enthusiasm. He avoided looking at Naomi as he walked to the other side of the bed, yet he was fully aware of her presence. Of the scent of her perfume, different than the sweet lavender she used to wear.

Brittany reached out and held his hand, becoming a bridge between him and Naomi as she looked from one to the other.

"So that means you don't have to come to class today or tomorrow," Brittany added. "I know you didn't want to."

"I would have come," he assured her.

"But now you don't have to and you can get the stuff done on the house like you wanted too." Brittany turned to Naomi. "Jess is building his own house. He bought a place with an old house and is now building a new one right by it. Can't figure out why he would do that when he and his mom have this awesome place on the other side of the valley that they both own. That house is ginormous. Have you seen it?"

"Actually, I have," Naomi said with a reserved smile. She looked across the bed at Jess and in her eyes she caught a hint of puzzlement. As if she, too, was wondering why he thought he needed another home.

A lab tech came into the room rescuing him from explaining something to her she didn't need to know.

"I'm sorry," the tech said, glancing from one to the other as she set her tray of vials on the bedside table. "But I need to draw some blood for blood tests."

"Again?" Brittany complained. "I hate those. They hurt."

"We'll wait outside the room," Naomi said, patting Brittany on her shoulder. "You'll be fine, honey."

Then she walked past Jess and out the door. Jess gave Brittany a quick smile to encourage her, then followed Naomi. She stood outside in the hallway, her arms folded over her chest, glancing up at the sunlight pouring in through the skylight overhead as if drawn to the light. The sun caught the reddish highlights in her hair, burnishing it to a brownish-copper. Her hair was darker than it used to be and now it flowed over her shoulders halfway down her back.

She didn't look at him, though.

Jess rocked back and forth on his heels, trying to find the right thing to say, frustrated at how easily his old attraction to her surged from his past into the present.

"So I guess you'll be working for me," he said, needing to break the silence. Then he mentally rolled his eyes. Brilliant. That sounded positively feudal.

"I guess." Naomi drummed her fingers against her arms. "I know you didn't want me, but—"

"Please, let's not go back there." Jess felt a mixture of embarrassment and shame over his reaction to Dr. Brouwer's suggestion that he hire Naomi. "When I said that I was feeling overwhelmed...seeing you again...."

"I'm sure you were. It was a dramatic moment after Brittany's collapse at Mug Shots," she said, thankfully ignoring his last comment. She tapped her fingers some more, then finally looked over at him. "Just curious about your mom. Will she be involved at all?"

Jess stifled a cynical laugh. "My mother is, according to her, unable to deal with Brittany because she is still grieving the loss of her husband. Never mind that Brittany is still dealing with losing a father." He couldn't keep the bitter tone out of his voice. Even though he felt bad for his mother, he was frustrated and upset with her selfishness. "So, no, I don't think she'll be in the picture, which is typical."

Naomi held his gaze a moment, the hint of pity in her eyes creating a prickle of annoyance. He had often shared his frustration with his absent parents and his subsequent loneliness with her. She knew that behind his frustration with his mother lay a deeper sorrow that he had hinted at in their long talks together.

But now, in spite of his parents' lack of involvement in his life, or maybe because of it, he had become an independent person. He had inherited the ski hill from his father and had turned it around from a failing business to a successful venture. He wasn't the needy young man she had tutored. He didn't need or want her pity.

"I understand," was all Naomi said. "So let's discuss Brittany."

"Yes, good idea." He slid his hands in the back pockets of his blue jeans, shooting her a quick glance. "I was supposed to come for classes this afternoon on how to take care of her. I'm hoping I don't need to anymore."

Naomi shook her head. "No. I know what needs to be done, though I will come in tomorrow to the hospital to finalize her care plan. Do you know when she'll be discharged?"

"Dr. Brouwer was saying something about Tuesday."

"Okay, then. I'll come to the house tomorrow to have a look at how you've got things laid out for Brittany and we can take it from there." She kept her voice brisk and professional, and her confidence reassured him that Brittany was in good hands.

Her detachment created a distance that he was thankful for. She was trained to take care of people. To her this was a job. Nothing more. If she could see it that way, then so could he.

"You may as well know the house is not in the best of shape," he said. "It's an older house I bought for the property while I built my own place. I didn't figure on having a pregnant teenager come and stay."

Naomi held her hand up to stop him mid-apology. "I'm not coming to inspect it. Just to see how we can set things up for Brittany to make her room more accessible."

Jess nodded, realizing how defensive he sounded. He wasn't sure why he felt he had to justify his current living conditions to Naomi when, as Brittany said, a ginormous house sat close by. Maybe it was because he remembered how impressed Naomi was by his parents' home. She especially loved the grand room, as his mother liked to call it, with windows soaring three stories up and overlooking Rockyview and the mountains beyond. Naomi would stand by the window and look down into town trying to find the apartment she shared with her mother and her sisters.

He didn't need to explain his desire to have his own house. To start his own place free from the dark and heavy memories of the house he grew up in. He had wanted to sell it, but his mother owned half of it. So they rented it out instead.

Naomi took a breath, then turned to him, her smile apologetic. "By the way, I was sorry to hear about your father's death. I know it was a while ago, but I'm sorry I didn't send a card or anything. Billy said I should have, but I just...I felt like it wasn't my place. I know you weren't close to your father, but I'm sure it was still difficult."

Jess rocked back on the heels of his boots as he acknowledged her sympathy with a curt nod, preferring not to talk about his father right now. Like his relationship with Naomi, he, too, was part of a past he was trying to move on from.

"Thanks for that," was all he said.

An awkward quiet fell between them after his acknowledgment of her apology, then, thankfully, the lab tech came out of the room, giving them both a quick smile. "All done in there. You can go in now."

Jess nodded and as the lab tech bustled away, vials rattling in her carrier, he took a step toward Brittany's room. "I should go in and visit with Brittany. So I'll see you tomorrow?"

Naomi nodded, wrapping her arms around her midsection as she held his gaze. She looked so dispassionate, so calm, it was as if the turbulent emotions that had overcome them both so long ago had been eased away by time.

And wouldn't they? After all, she'd had Billy to help her in the forgetting.

He'd had no one.

Well, this was it.

Naomi parked her car in front of Jess's house, pulled down the visor and checked her makeup in the mirror.

The hair was okay. The serviceable ponytail made her look more professional, she thought. Never mind that the ponytail drew attention to eyes made overlarge by the hollowness of her cheeks.

According to her sister Hailey she could use a haircut, but then according to her sister, she should do anything *but* go to work for Jess Schroder.

Naomi decided not to listen to Hailey on either count. She was doing this for Brittany and it was a good way to get more experience if that part-time job came up at the hospital.

Naomi slapped the visor up and stepped out of the car.

Before she went to the house, she took a moment to look over her shoulder at the town below her, nestled in the valley. Rockyview, British Columbia.

She had lived here until she graduated from high school. All during grade twelve she and Billy, her boyfriend since junior high school, had made plans to leave. He was studying to be a minister, she was taking an arts degree, which hopefully, would turn her love of stained glass into more than a hobby. Then, that fateful summer, Billy changed plans. He suddenly decided he was going on a mission trip and before he left, to Naomi's shock and surprise, he broke up with her. His rationale was that he thought she would be a distraction to him. He needed to focus on the Lord's work.

She was brokenhearted. Then she got the summer job tutoring Jess Schroder, son of the man who owned Rockyview Ski Hill and various other enterprises.

Jess had done poorly in most of his classes despite repeating them for another year.

Instead of focusing on his schoolwork, Jess had spent his time touring the countryside with his newest car, paid for by his parents, usually some girl from school accompanying him. Now he stood a good chance of not being able to go to college. So to help him write his college entrance exams, Naomi was hired to tutor him. Reluctantly she took the job, concerned about Jess's wild reputation. Her sisters warned her and so had Nana, but the money was too good to pass up.

Jess was so far behind, he needed help in every subject, so they spent every day together. Then, in spite of missing Billy, Naomi did what every other girl in Rockyview had done. She fell in love with Jess Schroder. And, to her amazement, he claimed he fell in love with her. They started dating, spending every spare moment together. She taught him to buckle down and practice self-discipline. He taught her to take risks, to live life. To enjoy herself. They shared kisses up on the tops of mountains, at the edges of quiet pools hidden in the hollows of the hills. They shared confidences, they made plans as they tore around the countryside in Jess's car. Then, one night, alone in his parents' house across the valley, they made love.

Naomi slammed a mental door on those memories. She knew she was flirting with disaster by accepting this job, but she also knew that to move on, she had to get through this.

Think of Billy and what he did for you, she reminded herself, drawing out another set of memories. A picture of Billy's friendly smile. His kind eyes. His gentle nature.

A gust of wind surged up from the valley and up the mountain and she wrapped her sweater more snugly against the sudden chill as she turned away from the town and her memories.

Even though Jess had prepared her, she was still surprised to see the peeling shingles and faded siding painted an anemic pink. Old Mr. McNab, an elderly man who used to own the flower shop in town, used to own this house. But he sold the house and property to Jess and the flower shop to Mia Verbeek. One of the many changes that happened in Rockyview while she was gone.

As she walked up the cracked and broken sidewalk to the house, the ringing sound of hammers and saws echoed over the valley from the larger home that was in the process of being built a couple of hundred yards away.

She glanced at her watch. She said she would meet Jess here at about four. She was early but knocked on the door nonetheless.

To her surprise she heard heavy footfalls, then the door opened and there was Jess. Sawdust was sprinkled through his hair and on the shoulders of his shirt and today a dark stubble shadowed his lean jaw.

She just wished her heart wouldn't falter each time she saw him.

Give it time, she consoled herself. *Keep remembering why you broke up.*

"So why don't you come in?" he asked, pulling the creaking screen door open and standing aside.

She stepped into the house and as the door closed behind her, she looked around the room.

A large, worn and overstuffed couch perched under the window and beside it sat a cracked leather recliner. Opposite that was a futon that had seen better days before she was born. She couldn't help comparing it to the house Jess and his parents used to live in.

Jess's former home had been located on the other side of the mountain that held Rockyview Ski Hill. It had been built to impress, and it did. The first time she'd gone inside she'd gotten turned around and actually got lost. Naomi could still remember how her voice used to echo in the vastness of that cold, often empty house the first few weeks she was tutoring Jess. It was beautiful but always felt empty to her.

"Told you it wasn't much," Jess said, his tone apologetic. "Come, I'll show you where Brittany is staying."

Naomi followed him down a dark, narrow hallway and into a small room containing a double bed and the detritus of a teenage girl's life.

"It took her only a week to transform my storage room into this nest," Jess said as he picked up a sweater from the floor and laid it on a chair already full of clothes. The sweater fell off the pile, he picked it up and tried again.

The room's walls held a few posters, and some family pictures in frames jockeying for space on a long shelf with stuffed animals, candles and brightly colored tins. Scarves and necklaces hung from hooks on the wall and were draped over the lamp beside a bed overflowing with pillows.

"It helps that she's on the main floor," Naomi said looking around the room. "Does she read?"

"Magazines," Jess said, his hands on his hips as he surveyed the room with a disgruntled look that in spite of her heightened awareness of him, made her smile.

"You might want to think about putting in a television for her so she can have something else to do," Naomi suggested.

"That's no problem. I can hang one on the wall here," Jess said, grimacing at the poster pasted up on the wall behind him. "It wouldn't break my heart to take Justin Bieber's or One Direction's grinning mugs down."

"Where is the bathroom?"

"Right across the hall." Jess gestured. "It's been taken over, too. Curling irons, makeup and enough hair stuff to start a beauty salon."

Naomi laughed at his comment, which netted her a quick glance.

Jess's mouth curved in a slow-release smile and his eyes held hers.

She couldn't look away and for a moment it was as if time circled backward. Naomi felt her breath catch in her throat as old emotions rose up between them, palpable and frighteningly real.

She swallowed and jerked her head away. "What about your mother? Has she been staying here?"

"No, she's been staying at her condo in Calgary. Soothing her broken heart." He sounded cynical and Naomi didn't blame him. She couldn't believe that Sheila would leave this young girl on her own and in such dire straits. But then the cup of human kindness only held a few drops for Sheila Schroder slash whatever she was called these days.

"So why did your mother bring her to Rockyview if she isn't staying?" Naomi asked.

"She had just found out that Brit was pregnant and she flipped. Guess the father didn't want to get involved. So she brought her here, hoping I could help out." He released a harsh laugh. "As if I can be any kind of influence on her. I'm not her brother and I'm certainly not father material."

Naomi's heart twisted at his words. "You still think that?" she asked quietly, as old memories rose attached to old pain. And behind that came the ruinous emotions of the fight they had over this very issue. She'd thought he loved her. Thought after becoming intimate they would become more serious. She had hinted at commitment and family, but Jess shut her down with the same words he spouted now. How he didn't want to be a father. He wanted an easygoing life without the trouble of kids. She'd felt betrayed and the words, angry and hurtful, were lobbed like grenades between them. In the end their relationship could not stand up under the conflagration.

"I'm not, Naomi," he said, holding her steady gaze. "I don't lie. What you see is what you get. I'm not the kind of guy who's made to be a father. I'm not...I'm not your kind of guy."

Deep sadness followed on the heels of her anger and with it came the comments from her sisters in letters and phone calls over the past few years. Jess dating this girl, then that girl and, after a while, Naomi stopped asking. Jess was who he was. He wasn't changing.

Then why did it still affect her so much?

CHAPTER 3

"*W*hy don't you stay overnight tonight?" Brittany fiddled with her blanket, twisting it around her fingers. "It gets pretty quiet here and I get lonely."

Naomi folded Brittany's sweater and laid it in the dresser drawer, shooting the young girl a smile. "Jess isn't that far away. All you have to do is call him on your phone. Or text him. Or yell, for that matter."

"Don't know why he figures he has to stay at the other house. It's not even finished." Brittany picked up one of the new gossip magazines Naomi had bought for her and paged listlessly through it as Naomi finished putting away the last of the laundry.

Naomi was finishing up her second day on the job and ever since she'd started, Brittany had been campaigning for her to stay the night. Something Naomi was fairly adamant she wouldn't do.

"Okay, that's the last of the clothes. I've laid out supper for you and Jess. I've already laid out your portions. Make sure you eat it all," Naomi said with a warning frown as she pushed the drawer closed. "The amounts I'm giving you won't make you fat. Besides, you need to eat enough for the baby."

Brittany put her hand over her stomach, as if to remind herself that yes, this mound under her clothes was, indeed, a baby.

"I don't feel like eating," Brittany said with a sigh.

"Doesn't matter what you feel like, you have to think about your baby," Naomi warned her. She and Brittany had had this same conversation at lunchtime when the girl didn't want to eat the soup Naomi had made. So Naomi had made a sandwich, and Brittany had scarfed it down by the time Naomi returned from taking the soup to the kitchen. "Besides, if you don't eat, you'll get an insulin reaction."

"Yeah, yeah, I know," she said, waving off Naomi's concerns.

"So what was your last blood test?"

Naomi had been trying to get Brittany involved in her own care and had shown her how to do the blood tests today.

"It was good," Brittany said, giving her the number.

"And your blood pressure is good, so we're set. Make sure you do another blood test before supper. We have to keep monitoring that to make sure you're getting the right balance between your diet and insulin." Naomi would have preferred to get the girl on an insulin pump, but Brittany had fought against that. So until then, Naomi needed to do constant calculations based on her blood sugar and her diet. She was also trying to get Brittany to take charge of her condition.

Naomi looked around the room. She had tidied and cleaned and now there was nothing left to do. "I set up your online account to stream movies so you're ready to go. Just in case, there's a DVD player as well. So I'm leaving now."

Brittany slumped back in her bed, her expression morose. "My DVD player doesn't work."

Naomi frowned. "Sure it does. You said you used it last night."

"I don't know what's happening. It wasn't working this morning before you came. Can you get Jess to come here and have a look at it?"

"Why don't you stream some shows instead?"

"The internet is really spotty. Jess told me that he didn't want to upgrade. Don't know why, he's got tons of money."

"Okay. I'll see what I can do." After their last conversation she and Jess had managed to avoid each other for the most part. He spent every day at the new house, working inside. She saw him from time to time when he came to this house for something to eat, but their last conversation was a good reminder to her to keep her distance. Not that she had to worry about that. Jess seemed to be helping her keep her resolution by staying away himself.

"I'll go talk to Jess," she said. "And I'll see you tomorrow."

She gave Brittany a quick pat on the shoulder, grabbed her purse and then left the room.

The sun was still warm this late in the afternoon and she lifted her face to it, reveling in the late-summer heat. She should take Brittany outside tomorrow. Let her enjoy the sunshine.

There were no trucks parked by the house. *The other workers must be gone for the day,* she thought as she walked up the driveway toward it, yet she heard the sound of a hammer.

Jess was still working.

She took a breath to silence her quickening heartbeat as she stepped into the house. The smell of fresh-cut wood and sawdust assailed her senses as she walked into the foyer and turned a corner into the house itself.

The walls weren't painted yet and she saw footprints in the sawdust and plaster dust coating the floor. But light spilled into the room coming from the floor-to-ceiling windows dominating the wall to her right.

She had to smile at the sight as she tried to imagine what this house would look like finished.

The room with the windows jutted out from the rest of the house. Soaring two stories above her, she saw an open-beamed ceiling finished off with wood. At the far end of the room, a curved staircase flowed upward to a railed walkway. As she wandered farther, she saw a bay window that, she guessed, would be part of the dining room and beside that, pipes jutted out of a wall that were probably part of the kitchen.

She made a slow circle wondering, again, why a man who didn't seem ready to settle down was building such a large home.

"Can I help you?"

The voice made her jump. Naomi looked up to see Jess looking down at her, one hand on the railing, the other still holding his hammer.

"Brittany was wondering if you could come and look at her DVD player. She said it doesn't work."

Jess nodded and then glanced at the watch on his wrist. "Sure. May as well quit for the day." He dropped his hammer into the tool belt circling his hips, then jogged down the stairs, raising little poofs of dust.

"This is a beautiful house," Naomi said.

"Getting there," Jess returned, pulling a hanky out of his back pocket and wiping the dust off his face.

Naomi only nodded, wishing her pulse didn't quicken around him. Even with Billy she'd never felt this sense that she couldn't quite catch her breath.

She headed blindly toward the door, then stumbled over the board she had stepped over when she came in. She would have fallen, but Jess caught her by the arm, steadying her and pulling her back upright.

For a moment they stood close enough that she could see the tiny wrinkles fanning out from his eyes, the faint scar on his cheek that he got when he was learning to ride a bike. She swallowed down her unwelcome reaction to his nearness and with a murmur of thanks, she drew away.

Why did this man still affect her so, she wondered as she turned away from him, this time walking with more care.

She reminded herself that she was in charge of her emotions and of her heart. She wasn't going to let herself be pulled into a relationship again.

"I'll see you at the house," was all she said, then turned and walked away.

Jess toed off his scuffed and scarred work boots, set them on the wooden floor of the porch, then dropped his tool belt beside them. He shoved his hand through his hair, releasing a shower of sawdust. He had managed to keep his distance from Naomi for the past couple of days. Seeing Naomi reminded him repeatedly that he was nothing like Billy, and he'd had enough of that soul-destroying comparison in his life. How often had his father told Jess he would never amount to much? That he was nothing like he was when his father was Jess's age.

Please, Lord, he prayed, *I want to move on. Help me to do this. You promised me.*

He pulled in a breath and glanced out the window at Naomi who was heading down the rutted driveway toward her car. Probably making sure not to fall again. He smiled to himself.

"Jess? Jess?" Brittany's voice called out.

"Coming." He brushed off the remainder of the sawdust, then walked into the house.

"Jess." A note of panic in her voice made him hurry his steps. When he came into the room, Brittany was lying on her side. Sweat beaded her forehead and her face looked unnaturally pale.

Jess panicked. What was going on?

"I feel funny. Like I did...like I did before...." her voice faded away and she blinked a long, slow blink as a trickle of sweat dripped down her face.

This did not look good, but he didn't know what to do. Naomi. Was she gone yet?

"I'll be right back," he said, then charged out of the room, down the hall and out the door. Naomi was standing by her car, her hand on the doorframe. It looked as if she was staring at the new house.

"Naomi, thank goodness you haven't left yet," he called out. "Something's wrong with Brittany."

Naomi slammed her door shut and quickly ran up the walk. "What's wrong?"

"I don't know." He headed back to the bedroom, Naomi, thankfully, was right behind him.

Brittany lay on the bed, and as Jess came into the room, she gave him a wan smile which grew when she saw Naomi. "Hey."

"How are you feeling now?" Naomi asked as she hurried to Brittany's side.

"Terrible. I feel all yucky and wobbly. I'm shaky and I can't keep my eyes focused."

"Insulin reaction," Naomi said, turning to Jess. "I need pop. Or something sweet to drink. Or a chocolate bar."

Jess jumped off the bed and once again was tearing down the hallway. He yanked open the fridge and grabbed a couple of cans of pop and a carton of juice. Then ran back to Brittany's bedroom, the concern on Naomi's face hurrying his steps.

Naomi was on the other side of the bed, opening her nurse's bag. She looked up when he came into the room. "She needs to get that down, if possible," she said.

"How much is she supposed to drink?" Jess asked, snapping open the tab of a pop can. He glanced at Brittany, alarmed at how white she had become. She was sweating as hard as if she'd been swinging a hammer all day.

"All of it," Naomi said, her tone curt, which made Jess realize how serious this was.

As Naomi supported Brittany, Jess raised the pop to her lips. "C'mon, Brittany. Drink this down."

Brittany took a sip, then made a face. "It's too sweet."

"It's supposed to be. You need the sugar," Naomi insisted in a firm voice as she lifted Brittany's finger and poked something into the tip of it. "Take another sip."

"That hurts." Brittany cried, pulling away, pop spilling down the front of her T-shirt.

Jess glanced over at Naomi. "Did she have enough?"

"Just keep making her drink," Naomi said, her mouth set in grim lines as she squeezed a drop of blood onto a small strip then put it in a small machine. "I'll tell you when to stop, but as long as she can keep drinking, keep going."

So Jess did as he was told, surprised to see such determination in a person he had always thought of as so sweet and gentle.

Brittany tried to push his hand away, but Jess, feeling like a bully, made her swallow down some more.

"C'mon, Brit. A couple more sips, honey. Please."

She looked at him and to his surprise, he saw the glimmer of tears in her eyes.

"What's wrong?" he asked.

"You called me honey," she said, sounding surprised.

"Yeah, well. I say that to all the girls," he joked, feeling uncomfortable around the emotions of a girl he barely knew. "Drink some more and I might call you sweetie. Or sugar plum." Thankfully his teasing worked and she took a few more mouthfuls.

"This is the worst stuff," she said, blinking. "Who in the world drinks root beer?"

Naomi frowned as the little machine she held beeped and some numbers flashed on the small screen. "Just as I thought.

It's low. Hopefully we won't need to give her glucagon." She looked over at Brittany. "You have to drink it all."

Brittany rolled her eyes and with a heavy sigh, took the can of pop in her hand, tipped her head back and gulped it down. Then she grimaced and lay back on the pillows piled up behind her head. "There. Satisfied?" she said, handing Jess the can and shooting Naomi an angry glance. "I'll probably gain like ten pounds from all that sugar and have some kind of hyperactive baby."

"You did good," he said, "but I don't think you have to worry about your weight or the baby." He took the empty can, surprised to see his hand shaking. He clenched the can, drew in a steadying breath, then glanced over at Naomi who shot him a grateful smile.

"Thanks for your help," she said.

He wanted to say more, but then Brittany groaned and Naomi's attention was turned back to her.

"My head," Brittany muttered, her hands clutching her temples. "It's so sore."

"You'll have a cracking headache because of the reaction," Naomi said. "I'll get you some pain killers."

Jess stood back as Naomi went into a large, black bag she had taken with her. She pulled out a container of pills and gave Brittany some. Then handed her a bottle of water. Naomi brushed her hip against the end table as she bent over Brittany. The table wobbled and the lamp on it would have fallen off, but Naomi caught it. Then she bent over and picked up a plate holding a sandwich. "You didn't eat your lunch," she said quietly.

Brittany looked away and shook her head.

"And I suppose your blood tests weren't what you said either."

"I hate blood tests, but now I have a headache."

"From not doing what I told you," Naomi said. "I'll pull the curtains." Naomi walked over to the window to draw the curtains. Or tried to.

"Here, I'll take care of that," he said, feeling a flush of embarrassment at the slapdash window coverings. This room wasn't supposed to be inhabited by anyone. He'd kept his bike, snowboard and other sports equipment here for storage. It was never supposed to be a bedroom.

"It's okay. I've nailed up curtains before," she said with a wry note in her voice.

Jess brushed past her. He caught the one end of the bed sheet and dragged it across the window and hooked it on the other end of the curtain rod.

The makeshift curtain dimmed the light a little and Brittany eased down into the bed, her eyes drifting closed.

Naomi shifted the blankets over Brittany, then, gathering up her things, left the room, Jess following.

"So what happened in there?" Jess asked when they got to the kitchen. "Why was she supposed to drink that pop? I thought diabetics weren't supposed to have sugar?"

"Brittany was having an insulin reaction," Naomi said. "What that means is her blood sugar had fallen to a dangerously low level and to bring it up she needed to have a huge influx of sugar. She got the reaction because she didn't eat her lunch and she didn't do the blood test I told her to." Naomi bit her lip and shook her head as if frustrated.

"Is she going to be okay?"

"She'll sleep for a while now. Anytime a diabetic has an insulin reaction, they are usually tired and often have a bad headache. So I'll leave her for a little while, then go and check her blood sugar again. The pop will have done the trick, but I'll need to keep an eye on her."

Jess blew out a sigh as he shoved his hand through his hair, pushing it away from his face, his hand still trembling. He'd done many crazy things in his life and had a number of close calls, but it was always his own life on the line. Never anyone else's.

"That was scary," he said. "Will that happen again?"

"Not if she eats on time and does regular blood tests."

"So what about tonight? What if it happens again tonight?"

Naomi sighed and bit her lip. "I don't know."

"I can't take care of her. I'm staying in the other house." Jess blew out a sigh, his heart still pounding in reaction.

"You have another bedroom in this house, don't you?"

Jess nodded. "Just across the hall from Brittany's. There's also another one upstairs, though it's full of the stuff I pulled out of Brittany's room."

"I could stay the night, if you want. Just to keep an eye on her."

Relief sluiced through Jess. "Yeah, that'd be great."

Not ideal, but it took some pressure off him.

Naomi pressed her fingers to her forehead, as if thinking. "I have to go to town to get a few things, but I'll be back in about an hour."

"Will she be okay?"

"For an hour, yes. The pop she drank will tide her over. I'll check her when I get back."

She looked up and gave him a wan smile. "I know this isn't ideal, but it's the best thing for Brittany if I stay overnight."

Her reluctance battered at his own defenses. He knew this was the last thing she wanted, but then, so did he.

This was for Brittany. He could deal with this for Brittany's sake. Once his mother got her act together, she would be back and she would take care of her responsibilities again.

In the meantime, he had to keep his distance. He couldn't afford to let Naomi too close, after all the years he'd spent building up the walls around his heart.

CHAPTER 4

*W*here was she?

Naomi lay perfectly still, her eyes adjusting to the darkness of the room as she struggled to orient herself. Then Naomi caught a glint of light coming through a window in the wrong place in the wall and reality seeped into her sleep-fogged brain.

This was Jess's room and Brittany was right across—

Brittany.

Insulin reaction.

Naomi bolted upright in the bed, grabbed her robe and tossed it on over her pajamas. She belted it as she hurried out of the room to Brittany's across the hall.

The young girl lay curled up on her side, blankets twisted around her, one hand resting palm up beside her head, her dark hair covering her face. Her lips held a faint smile, as if she was having good dreams.

Naomi touched her forehead, but her skin was dry and cool.

The tension in her shoulders eased as she looked down at the sleeping girl, then she walked to the window, easing it open. The sun was coming up over the mountains, spilling its rosy light over the valley and onto Brittany's bed. The day promised to be a beautiful one.

Naomi's gaze wandered over the mountains unconsciously, seeking the figure of the Shadow Woman. It was too early in the day to see her, but she and her sisters would often try to puzzle out her location before the afternoon sun brought her features out.

According to Bond family lore, the Shadow Woman was waiting for her lost love to return. When the light was right, the rocks and ledges created a picture of a face leaning forward, as if looking for him.

Sometimes Naomi felt like that woman, living in the shadows of her exuberant younger sister, Hailey, and her capable older one, Shannon. Even her relationship with Billy was like a shadow of a real one. Engaged for so long, never married. Never sharing more than a chaste kiss.

"How is she doing?"

The deep voice behind her made Naomi jump. She spun around, pushing her hair back from her face to see Jess, already clothed, standing in the doorway. He had shaved and his hair still held the damp sheen of his shower.

Naomi tried not to feel self-conscious about her lack of makeup, her disheveled hair, the ratty robe that had seen better days. She wrapped it tighter around herself, like a shield.

"She did okay," Naomi said, focusing on Brittany. "I checked her at about two again and her blood sugar was low, so I got her up to drink some more. I need to talk to Ben, Dr. Brouwer, about adjusting her insulin. I would prefer to get her on a pump. It would regulate her more." She forced herself to stop. She was talking too fast and too long. Nerves.

Jess didn't reply and, instead, came into the room and stood at the end of Brittany's bed. "She looks too young to be pregnant and have a kid," he said quietly. "She's just a kid herself."

Naomi pulled the covers around Brittany's shoulders, then

smoothed them down with a protective motion. Naomi wanted to ask about the status of the baby once it was born, but wasn't sure it was her right. Again, she wished Sheila was here to help Brittany through this difficult time. A girl needed her mother when life was hard like this.

"I have coffee made if you want some," Jess said.

Naomi caught a delightful whiff of coffee brewing and her mouth watered. "I'd love a cup," she said. "But first let me get dressed."

Once in her room, Naomi grabbed the clothes she had laid out the night before, then scooted into the bathroom.

She ran a brush through her hair, put on some eyeshadow and a hint of blush then pulled on her black pants and a light blue oxford shirt. Not quite a nurse's uniform, but at least it was somewhat professional-looking.

She chanced a look in the mirror, making a face at her hollow cheeks. Two weeks of waitressing at Mug Shots and indulging in Kerry's famous banana loaf still hadn't helped her put on the weight she'd lost the last year of taking care of Billy.

She paused a moment, her mind ticking back to her fiancé as if trying to remind herself of what she had lost. But all she could bring up was a picture of Billy lying on the bed in his parents' house, his cheekbones standing out in stark relief against his pale skin, his eyes dark shadows in his face.

Then, as if unable to stop herself, superimposed on that memory came a picture of Jess with his sparkling eyes, thick hair and broad shoulders, the picture of life and vitality.

Naomi caught herself up short. *Lord, please help me to honor Billy's memory,* she prayed. *Help me to stay true to a man who was there for me. Help me to figure out who I am and what I should be doing with my life.*

She drew in a breath as she let her prayer settle and become a part of her. Then, when she felt ready, she left the bathroom.

Jess was pouring a cup of coffee and looked up as Naomi

came into the room. "Do you still take two sugars in your coffee?"

"You still remember?" she said with a nod, surprised. Billy had never paid any attention to those kind of details. Every time he ordered her coffee at Tim Hortons, she always had to go back to get sugar.

Right behind that came a flicker of disloyalty. Billy was a good man. She had no right to compare him to Jess.

He shrugged off her question. "Lucky guess," he said as he handed her the mug.

She took it with a murmured thanks, then sat down at the kitchen table. To her surprise and dismay, he sat down across from her, his own coffee cup cradled between his palms. She thought he was returning to his house to work.

She wrapped her hands around the warm mug, realizing she was being foolish. From the way things were going with Brittany, she would be seeing Jess more often. Surely she could treat him the same as she would any other old friend?

"You sleep okay—"

"Do you stay—"

"Go ahead—"

They both spoke the same words at the same time, then both stopped.

Jess gave a light laugh and glanced her way and held out a fisted hand. "Rock, paper, scissors?"

As she held his gaze, it was as if time hurtled backward again and they were two young kids sitting in his car, parked at the lookout point overlooking Rockyview Valley. They'd never had a problem talking. Words flowed so easily between them, and every time they started talking at the same time, they played the game to see who got to go first.

"You always won," she said.

"That's because you were predictable."

She released a slow smile. "I don't know if that's a compliment or a put-down."

Jess's expression grew serious. "It wasn't a put-down."

"Okay." She took a quick sip of her coffee, then sputtered, covering her mouth with her hand. "That's really hot."

"You still can't wait until it cools off, can you?" he said, blowing on his own coffee.

Another silence rife with past memories rose between them.

He still knows so much about me.

The thought both disconcerted her and warmed her at the same time. She wasn't sure which emotion to connect with. She glanced out the window at the new house. That should be a safe topic.

"House is coming along?" she asked.

"Yeah. Got most of the plumbing done. So now it's painting and flooring and cabinets and the outside."

"So I'm curious," she said, "why are you building this place when you've got the other one? I understand you've been working on it for a few years."

Jess pursed his lips, as if wondering whether to answer her or not, then shrugged. "I bought this property with my own money and have been building the house as I could afford to. I wanted my own place where I could start fresh. A place full of light and peace."

The bare wood exterior of the house and the mounds of dirt pushed up beside the foundation showed how much work needed to be done, as he had said, before it would look like a home. "Your own memories?" she asked, latching on to his last comment. "As opposed to the ones you have from your other house?"

"I want a fresh start. That house holds memories I want to put behind me."

The time they had spent there—was that something he *also* wanted to put behind him?

She looked down at her coffee and sighed. Being around him was getting complicated and awkward. How was she supposed to get through this job?

As if sensing her own distraction, Jess pushed his own mug aside and rested his crossed forearms on the table. "You know, if you're going to be around this much we may as well get things out in the open."

She looked at him, not so sure she wanted to go to the place he was heading toward. "What do you mean?"

"We used to date. We spent a lot of time together and had a lot of fun and then we broke up. We decided we didn't really...you know..."

She waited, hoping he would finish, then she slowly shook her head. "I'm sorry, I don't know what we 'didn't really.'"

Jess angled his gaze away from her, then looked back, his dark eyes holding hers in an intense gaze. "Belong together."

Those two brutally honest words cut to the core of her being. She was surprised they could still hurt.

She drew in a deep breath. "Yes, we used to date," she said. "We were kids who got...carried away."

Jess nodded, looking down at his mug. "I always felt bad about what happened that night."

"Only bad?"

As soon as those words left her lips, she wished she could pull them back. She had come back to Rockyview to move on, to look ahead, to be in charge of her life.

Not to delve into the mistakes of her past. She wasn't allowing herself to be defined by a relationship with a man anymore. She was Naomi Deacon, and she was her own person.

Then Jess looked up at her, his eyes narrowed as if her question hurt him somehow. "I'm sorry, Naomi. I didn't mean to hurt you. I cared about you and I got carried away, like you said."

The only sound in the silence that followed was the hum of

the refrigerator and then, in the far distance, the lonely wail of the train that regularly rumbled through Rockyview. The silence swelled as the past reared up and hovered between them.

"But you did hurt my heart," Naomi couldn't help saying, her fingers tight on the handle of her mug as her emotions slipped, too easily, back to that dark time.

It was the end of summer. She knew she was leaving and Jess was talking about college. She was afraid that he would leave her behind.

The housekeeper, who Jess's parents had hired to supervise him, had left for an unsanctioned weekend holiday, leaving Jess and her alone. In love and unsupervised, they became intimate, and everything in her life had shifted.

Afterward they both acknowledged that they had gone too far and they promised each other it wouldn't happen again. It didn't, but in the aftermath, Naomi's feelings for Jess grew and intensified. He became her whole life. He took over every part of her mind and soul.

Jess held her gaze, then shook his head. "I'm sorry, Naomi. What we had...what we did..."

She held her hand up to stop him. "What we did was a mistake," she said, disappointed to hear her voice falter. "A mistake I only made once, thankfully. You were the only one—"

She bit off that comment. What was wrong with her? Why was she telling him this?

She pushed herself away from the table, but in her hurry, she stumbled.

Jess got up and reached out to steady her, his arm grasping hers. The warmth of his hand and his nearness sent her heart into overdrive.

Jess touched her once and it was as if all those years with Billy were swept away. Once again, she ran the risk of letting another man swallow her up.

She felt like she couldn't breathe. Couldn't think. She jerked her hand away and dropped her cup. Coffee spilled out and spread across the floor.

Jess grabbed a cloth and bent over to wipe up the spill just as she crouched down to pick up her mug. Their shoulders brushed and Naomi pulled back again.

Jess sat back on his heels and handed her the cloth. "Maybe you better finish up here," he said quietly.

Naomi set her cup on the table and, without looking at him, started wiping up.

Jess blew out a sigh. "I'm sorry," was all he said. Then he got to his feet. "You seem tense around me."

Naomi didn't reply to that, just kept focusing on the floor and the coffee she was trying to contain.

"I'm getting the feeling that it might be easier if I stay away."

He phrased the sentence in such a way as to give her an opportunity to negate that. She knew she was being foolish, but when she had moved to Rockyview, it was with the idea that she would try to get her feet under her. Try to live an independent life and not get swallowed up by feelings anymore.

Instead she was plunged into daily contact with him, which she was obviously not ready for.

She glanced up at him and nodded. "Maybe it would be," she agreed. Then a noise from Brittany's room drew Naomi to her feet.

Jess took the cloth from her. "I'll finish up here. You go see to Brittany."

Naomi gave him a curt nod, then left, trying not to hurry. She opened the door to Brittany's room, closing it behind her.

Brittany, however, lay on the bed, eyes closed, hand curled up beside her face. She must have cried out in her sleep.

Naomi leaned back against Brittany's door, her stomach doing somersaults as she scrabbled for composure.

You were the only one.

Why had she spilled that out?

But it was true. That one moment with Jess had both shaken her world and her basic belief system. He was her first and only, and seeing him again only served to bring back all those emotions—shame, grief, love.

Like cards shuffled in a deck, she went through them all and behind them was a primal fear. Jess was dangerous. He would pull her in again. She would lose herself in him. She had let Billy overwhelm her, change her. She had to know who she was. Being around Jess only confused her.

She covered her face with her hands, desperately scrambling for composure. Sorrow mingled with shame as her mind dipped back to those horrible moments when she had confronted Jess all those years ago.

She had come to him with fear choking her throat and yet, at the same time, a hopeful yearning. And he pushed her away.

Dear Lord, please let me get through these next few moments. Help me not to let that old relationship, those old mistakes, define me.

Part of her wanted to quit. To leave again. She had spent enough tears and emotions on the shame that overwhelmed her after Jess rejected her.

Thankfully Billy had taken her back in spite of everything. Now, dear, faithful Billy was gone and even by letting the emotions of that past seep into her life, she felt as if she was being unfaithful to the man who was so faithful to her.

Naomi glanced over at the bed. Brittany lay on her side, her hair spilling over the pillow, her one hand resting protectively on her stomach.

Even though she wanted nothing more than to leave, she knew Brittany depended on her and she couldn't leave her alone.

Naomi wondered what kind of mother Brittany would be. Her biological mother had died when she was young, and her stepmother was so caught up in her own grief, she didn't have time for the young girl when she needed a mother most. What kind of example of a mother's love did she have?

Naomi pulled the bedcovers protectively over the young girl, slipping back to her own mother's frequent absences. How Noelle had moved away from Rockyview when Naomi and Hailey were old enough to be left alone. Neither she nor her sisters had heard from her for a couple of months.

And what kind of mother would you be with your own distant and emotionally reserved mother as a role model?

Thankfully she didn't have to face that prospect. Not for a long time. But if the time came, she knew she would be clinging to the verse that had sustained her all through Billy's illness.

I can do all this through Him who gives me strength.

Right now, what she needed to do was to figure out who Naomi Deacon was.

She had spent so much time in the shadow of Billy's personality, then, later on, in the shadow of his illness. He had taken over her life.

And so had Jess.

She had to keep her mind on the job she was asked to do and put a lock on her heart. She was committed to taking care of Brittany and she would bring this job to completion.

She wasn't getting pulled into a relationship that would consume her again.

As the bedroom door of Brittany's room fell shut behind Naomi, Jess bent over to finish cleaning up.

You were the only one.

Naomi's words echoed in his mind.

He knew she was talking about that night when they were alone in his parents' house. That night when emotions took over common sense and things went too far.

Everything changed after that night. They made sure they were never alone. And, he thought, they grew closer. He'd thought she was The One. Then, six weeks later, Billy came back to town. And Naomi happened to pick that night to start talking about kids and family. He said he didn't want to be a father. She kept pushing him, as if she was looking for a reason to find fault with him. To find an excuse to do exactly what she did.

Run back to Billy.

Perfect Billy who probably wanted a dozen kids and would be a fantastic father and who had probably never done more than give her a chaste kiss good-night.

He walked to the sink and tossed in the cloth and the remains of Naomi's coffee, wishing his heart would settle down. What had happened was his own fault. He had foolishly thought talking about their shared past would ease the constant tension they seemed to feel around each other.

You were the only one.

He took a moment to compose himself, wishing for a second that he could just leave town. Head up to the hills. Go hiking. Push himself to the limits of his endurance like he used to when things got tough at home.

But he couldn't. He was anchored here by his business and now, by Brittany.

Naomi was as appealing as she had been before. Maybe even more, he thought as he stepped out of the house and strode up the hill.

Trouble was, he knew he couldn't afford to let her close again as he had before. They weren't meant to be together. That much he did know. As he told Naomi, it would be better if he kept his distance.

Thankfully he had the house to keep him busy. And maybe avoiding her by working on the house was a good thing. He'd been trying to get this project done for a couple of years. If he worked every day and every night and weekends, he might finally get this house done. Maybe he'd finally have a true home. But even as those words settled into his mind, another thought taunted him.

Would it be a home if he was by himself?

Didn't matter. He couldn't be around Naomi.

Naomi's very presence had catapulted him into a time of his life that had been the source of his greatest hope and his greatest pain.

CHAPTER 5

"I'm tired of being inside." Brittany tossed the magazine aside and lay back against the pillows of her bed. "I want to go outside. Go for a walk."

Naomi took a shirt out of the laundry basket and as she folded it she gave the girl a sympathetic smile. "Sorry, honey, you were spotting yesterday after you walked in the living room. You have to stay in bed for today."

Brittany heaved out a dramatic sigh and folded her arms across her middle. "And what's with Jess? I've hardly seen him since you came here. He eats his supper in the house and hardly comes to see me." She frowned, as if she sensed Naomi had something to do with it.

Even though Brittany was young, and lying in her bed every day, the girl didn't miss much. But since Jess started keeping his distance, it had become easier for Naomi to do her job. "I don't get it," Brittany continued. "I thought he would be happy to see you again. I mean, you used to date each other."

"Emphasis on *used to*."

"Anyway, I wish he would come back to the house. At least for supper. It's so boring here."

Naomi felt another flicker of guilt, then pulled another one of Brittany's T-shirts out of the basket to distract the girl. She held it up and shook her head. "Seriously, Brittany? Do you own a T-shirt without a rude slogan on the front?"

"They make me laugh," Brittany said.

"But you don't see them if you wear them."

"Okay, they make my friends laugh. They made Scott laugh."

This was the first time Brittany had mentioned any boy's name in front of her. "And Scott is..." Naomi prompted, her voice quiet.

Brittany lowered her eyes, her face shuttered. "Doesn't matter. That's done."

Why wouldn't she talk about him? Unfortunately it seemed Brittany wasn't ready yet. Naomi's heart ached for the young girl. She needed someone beside her, helping and supporting her.

Like Jess had.

Naomi pushed that thought aside. Jess made the choice to stay away himself. It wasn't up to her. Sheila was the one who should be here helping Brittany.

Brittany heaved a sigh and glanced outside. "Why can't I go outside? I want to see the house again. Jess showed me around when I first got here. I wish I could see what he's done since then." This was followed by another dramatic sigh.

Naomi felt an inkling of sympathy for her. Brittany had been grumpy and out of sorts all morning and Naomi knew it was because she was feeling cooped up. "You know what Dr. Brouwer said. No walking at all until things settle down."

"I am so tired of lying in this room." This was followed by a faint sniff, and as Naomi put the last of the girl's clothes away, she caught a glimmer of a tear in Brittany's eyes.

"How about a game of Scrabble?" Naomi had been teaching her how to play the board game, thinking it might help her with her vocabulary.

"I suck at Scrabble."

"Do you want me to read to you some more?"

This was followed by a vehement shake of her head. "Just give me my phone. I want to text my friends again. Maybe this time they'll answer back. I'd watch YouTube videos if Jess could be bothered to upgrade his internet."

Naomi unplugged the phone and handed it to her, and Brittany leaned back against the headboard, swiped the screen and frowned. "No one's answered any of my texts."

She flicked her thumbs over the screen, sending out another raft of messages.

"I'll make some lunch for you," Naomi said, picking up the magazines scattered over the girl's bed and setting them in a pile on the end table by the bed so they'd be within easy reach.

"I'm not hungry," Brittany muttered, looking at the screen as if willing even one of her friends to answer her. She brightened when her phone immediately tweeted back, signaling a message. But her smile faded away. "Jess won't even come to visit. Why not? What did I do wrong?"

Guilt twisted Naomi's heart at the anguish in the girl's voice. She knew exactly why Jess wasn't coming and it had more to do with her than with Brittany. She didn't realize how much Brittany had connected with Jess in such a short time. She would have to talk to Jess about coming to see her. Naomi didn't want to be the cause of Brittany's feelings of isolation.

"What about a grilled cheese sandwich?" she asked. It was almost lunchtime.

"I'm not hungry." Brittany tossed her phone aside and pulled her pillow over her head as if trying to block out anything more Naomi might have to say. "Just go away. I hate my life and I hate this baby. I wish it would go away."

"Don't wish that, honey," Naomi said, her heart contracting in anguish. "Don't ever wish that." She stroked Brittany's arm, trying to convey her sympathy, but Brittany jerked away from her, lost in her own self-pity.

Later on, Naomi brought the grilled cheese sandwich, but Brittany took only a couple of bites.

That night Brittany ignored her supper and Naomi was forced to make her drink some more sugar-laced fruit juice, which she said made her sick to her stomach.

Her blood sugars ranged all over the map, her blood pressure was also affected and Naomi suspected much of it was directly related to the mini-depression the girl had fallen into.

When Brittany was in bed, Naomi tried to call Sheila but was sent to voicemail. So she left a carefully worded message about how Brittany could use her support and help right now.

She put the phone down and as she washed up the dinner dishes, she looked out across the yard to the house. Jess stood on the deck, looking out over the valley, eating from a bowl. Cold cereal, she suspected. She should know. She lived on the same thing for the last few months Billy was alive when his parents were trying to get her to eat something. Anything.

She thought of Brittany, who hadn't eaten anything either and Naomi knew why. The girl felt alone and uncared for at a time when she needed family around her the most. Sheila was out of the question, which left Jess, who was staying away because of her.

"Get over yourself," she said, tossing aside the tea towel. "You need to grow up and get through this. Brittany needs Jess right now. You don't care about Jess anymore, so what's the problem?"

As soon as she made her decision to go talk to him, a bright yellow car drove up the driveway, then parked in front of Jess's new house. A young woman got out, her long blond hair catching the glow of the early evening sun. She waved, then picked her way across the dirt and up the wooden steps to the deck Jess stood on.

Naomi couldn't hear them, but could see the woman's easy smile, the way her hand rested on Jess's arm. *Of course,* she thought, almost laughing at her surprise at the sight. She had heard any number of times from her sisters how Jess had moved on. He was an attractive single man with a good income. Women would be interested in him.

And not you?

She'd had her time with Jess and she had allowed him to take over her life and her emotions. She wasn't letting that happen again.

But at the same time, she knew she wasn't talking to Jess about Brittany right now.

"So you've got a double sink here and a smaller one in the island." Connor LaCroix made a quick sketch on his notepad, then tucked his pencil behind his ear and pulled out a tape measure. Connor was a tall man, with broad shoulders that seemed to fill up the kitchen. "Do you figure on a conventional-sized stove or do you have something else in mind? I can move the cabinets if I have to."

"I had my eye on one of those stoves with the large burner down the middle. Gas, preferably. The alcove for the stove will have a water pipe to it and it will be bricked in." Gail had recommended the feature and when he saw pictures of it he liked it immediately.

Connor nodded as he pulled out his tape measure. "Sounds like some lucky lady is getting an awesome kitchen." He gave Jess a quick wink. "Heard that Gail's been stopping by quite often."

"She's an interior decorator. I've been getting some advice from her," Jess abruptly said.

"Is that what it's called?" Connor said, his voice holding a hint of sarcasm.

"So when you stain the wood tomorrow, I was thinking a dark walnut for the doors and a lighter maple for the cabinet frames," Jess replied, holding Connor's gaze with his own.

Connor just grinned, not fazed by his avoidance. "Gail told me that's what you thought." He pulled out the tape and handed one end to Jess as he glanced over Jess's shoulder.

Connor's smile grew and his posture shifted.

Now what? Frowning, Jess looked behind him to see what or who Connor was grinning at.

Naomi stood in the doorway of the kitchen area, her hands clasped in front of her, her hair pulled back in her usual pony-tail. Her gaze flicked from Jess to Connor, then back again as she shifted her weight.

You were the only one.

Jess shook off that insidious thought. Irrelevant, he reminded himself.

Then he wondered what she was doing here, when she seemed so relieved after he told her it would be best if he kept his distance.

"Hey there, Naomi," Connor said, tossing off a wave of his gloved hand. "I heard you were back in town. What brings you to this loser's house?" He shot Jess a knowing look, as if wondering exactly how many women made it a habit of coming by here.

"Good to see you, too, Connor," Naomi said. Then she glanced toward Jess. "I...I need to talk to Jess for a minute."

"Of course you do," Connor said, letting his tape measure return to its case with a loud snick. "I'll go upstairs to the master bedroom and double-check the measurements for the vanity for the en-suite bathroom. Don't want to have to cut into my cabinets." He gave Naomi a grin then thankfully left, his booted feet echoing on the stairs beside the kitchen.

"So what can I do for you?" Jess asked, resting his hands on his hips.

"It's Brittany," Naomi said, her gaze flicking everywhere but at him. "She's feeling so cooped up and she's not been eating. I'm worried about her. I think...I think she feels abandoned."

"Did you talk to my mother?" He had to ask, although he was fairly sure his mother wasn't going to be much help in this situation.

"I tried calling but didn't get an answer and when I called her cell phone I only got her voicemail."

Probably not picking up when she saw his home number, Jess thought, frustration shooting through him. Sure she was grieving, but so was Brittany. At the least they could share stories of the man they both lost.

"Do you want me to go down and talk to my mom face to face?" He would have preferred not to as Calgary was two hour's drive one way. He could do it if he had to.

"Actually, Brittany had mentioned you used to take her through the house before she was put on bed rest. So I was wondering if you would be willing to bring her up here. She said she wanted to see what you had done on the house and I think a change of scenery would do her a lot of good."

"She can't walk up here herself?"

Naomi shook her head. "Absolutely not. She would need to be carried."

"I guess I can do that." If the poor kid wanted to get out of the house, he could arrange that. "When do you want me to do this?"

"I was hoping for lunchtime. She hasn't been eating a lot and I thought I could use this little outing as a bribe."

"That could work. Connor will be gone and my other workers aren't showing until two o'clock." He'd have some time to spend with her.

"Thanks so much. Brittany will be happy to hear that."

Her words were so stilted, as if the conversation of the other day stood between them like a live thing.

And it did. Try as he might he couldn't forget what she had said and, even more important, why she felt the need to tell him.

Naomi turned, but before she left, she glanced around the interior of the house, a faint smile lifting her lips. "This will be a beautiful place, Jess."

He shouldn't care but her compliment warmed his heart. "I hope so."

Then he caught a frown puckering her forehead and he turned to see what seemed to bother her.

A stained-glass bird spun slowly in the window of the living room sending out shafts of blue, pink and yellow light. A sun catcher Naomi had made for him all those years ago. Connor had found it in Jess's room two days ago and had hung it up here as a joke. Jess hadn't bothered to take it down.

"You still have that," she said, a note of wonder in her voice.

"It was too pretty to throw away," he said, as if he had considered doing exactly that.

Naomi simply nodded as a melancholy smile drifted across her face. Was she remembering the afternoon she gave it to him and what had happened afterward?

"Do you do any stained-glass work anymore?" he asked, trying to dismiss memories that rose up every time he was with Naomi again.

She shook her head, a sorrowful look on her face. "I took an art course when I went to college, but Billy persuaded me to switch to something more practical."

"Like nursing." He couldn't help the faint note of disdain in his voice. Sounded like something Billy would do.

"Nurse's aide, actually. But that training got me this job which is paying my bills right now." She lifted her chin and held his gaze, as if defending what Billy had suggested.

"That's true, but who knows where you could have been if

you kept on going with your stained-glass work." Jess didn't need to argue her out of the choices she had made, but it bothered him to think that she had thrown away a talent she had been given. "You were good at what you did, Naomi. You did some amazing work. You should have continued. If you had, you might be able to do more than just pay bills."

Wonder flashed in her eyes. Then she blinked and it was gone. "Doesn't matter," she said slicing the air with her hand as if cutting off that thought. "That time for me has passed. I need to do what I need to do."

"You sound like Billy," he couldn't help saying.

A look of hurt passed over her face and Jess regretted his outburst. Billy had been her fiancé and a good man. He had no right to put him down.

"I heard that happens when you spend a lot of time with someone," she said in a choked voice.

He was being a boor, he realized. Naomi was still grieving the loss of a man who had been a larger part of her life than Jess had ever been.

"I'm sorry, Naomi. I didn't mean to hurt you. Billy was a good man. A better man than...than most."

A better man than me, he was about to say, but held that thought back.

Naomi's curt nod acknowledged his apology, then she left, her ponytail bobbing as she made her way down the rutted road toward the house.

Jess pushed out an angry sigh. Why did he always manage to say the wrong thing at the wrong time?

Story of his life with Naomi.

CHAPTER 6

"*I* think this is the perfect spot," Brittany said, a huge smile lighting up her face as Jess set her into the large wooden chair he had set on the deck. "I can see the main street of Rockyview from here."

"So you can," Naomi said, glancing down at the valley. Rockyview lay below them, tiny and complete.

Sunshine, warm and friendly, poured down from the sky. Summer was winding down and the mornings already held the faint chill that was the harbinger of fall. But this time of day, with the bright sun illuminating the green hills, it was hard to believe in a few months these same hills would be dazzling white with snow.

Naomi set the tray of sandwiches down on the end table beside Brittany, thankful to see a smile on the young girl's face. "So I'll pour you some milk and then leave you and Jess alone," she said as she reached for her glass.

Brittany grabbed her hand. "No, stay here. I don't want you to go."

The sliding door behind them grumbled open as Jess stepped out carrying a couple of chairs. He plunked one down on one side of Brittany and brushed it off as best as he could. "Have a seat, Naomi. Sorry about the mess. That plaster dust settles everywhere."

So much for going back. It would look rude now.

"So what do we have here?" Jess asked, inspecting the sandwiches as he set his own chair on the other side of Brittany.

"Ham and cheese," Brittany was saying, pointing out the different sandwiches. "Egg salad for me and one with turkey, cheese and cranberry sauce."

"Wow, sounds a lot better than the peanut butter and jam one I was going to have." Jess flashed Naomi a quick smile, but she could see tension edging his mouth. He was putting on a good show for his stepsister.

Well, if he could she could, she thought, settling down into the chair.

She picked up the jug of milk she had taken as well and poured some for Brittany, then handed her a napkin.

Brittany took a sandwich and was about to take a bite when Jess pulled off his hat and rested his elbows on his knees.

"I...uh, thought we could pray before lunch," he said, almost apologetically.

Naomi, who was reaching for a sandwich herself, could only stare, then she felt a quietening in her soul. Even though his parents went to church from time to time, Jess had never wanted to attend with her. He had always spouted the usual mishmash of how the church was full of hypocrites and he didn't want any part of that.

She had never dared challenge him on that. She was so young herself, still finding her own way through faith. But it had bothered her and had introduced a tension she could never reconcile.

A tension she never felt with Billy.

But here was Jess, his hat dangling between his hands, his

eyes holding hers, asking if he could pray a blessing over sandwiches.

"He always does this," Brittany whispered, as if apologizing for her stepbrother's quirks.

"This is a good thing to do," Naomi said with a gentle smile. Then she bowed her head, as well.

Jess said a quick blessing on the food, thanking the Lord for the beautiful day and for the many blessings they had. He prayed for Brittany and her baby. Then he paused a moment, as if adding his own silent prayer.

Naomi felt a surprising peace wash over her as Jess prayed, and in the silence following his prayer, she added one of her own.

Help me, Lord, to know what I'm supposed to do here. Help me to know who I am and what I want.

Then she lifted her head, looking across the space at Jess, who, she was surprised to see, was looking at her.

"Thanks for that," she said quietly. Then she poured Brittany a glass of milk and took a sandwich for herself.

A comfortable silence rose between them as they ate and Naomi was surprised to feel a release of the tension that had been an unwelcome visitor and their constant companion.

An answer to her prayer?

Behind them Naomi could hear the buzz of a saw. Connor was working on the cabinets in the kitchen and had refused the offer of lunch. Said he wanted to get done as much as possible, so he was still working.

"It's so awesome to be outside," Brittany said, wiping her mouth with the napkin Naomi had provided. She sat back in her chair and shifted as if to make room for the baby. She grimaced a moment, but then as she sat back, a smile shining on her face. "I love this."

"Are you feeling okay?" Naomi asked anyway, needing to make sure.

"I feel great right now." Brittany gave Jess a shy smile, but he was leaning back in his chair, his booted feet crossed at the ankles as he ate his sandwich.

"Do you want more?" Naomi asked, thankful that Brittany was finally eating.

Brittany nodded and Naomi got up to get it for her.

"Hey, what's that?" Brittany asked pointing to Naomi's neck.

"What's what?"

"That necklace. Around your neck. How did I not see it before?" Brittany asked, taking the sandwich from Naomi.

Naomi glanced down, lifting the gold nugget attached to a chain. "This? I got this from my grandmother. My nana Bond."

"It looks like gold."

"It's one of five gold nuggets that have been passed down through the family. Once this one was part of a bracelet my nana used to wear." Naomi tucked her chin as she lifted the gold nugget to look at it even though she knew its contours by heart. As a young girl she would sit on her grandmother's lap and toy with her bracelet.

"There's a story attached to those nuggets, isn't there?" Jess said.

He remembered? Naomi was fairly sure she had told him only once when he had seen Nana's bracelet and was curious about it.

"Tell me the story," Brittany demanded.

"Please," Jess added, giving Brittany a gentle tap on her shoulder. He added a smile to show he was teasing. Brittany pulled a comical face, then turned back to Naomi.

"My brother is trying to teach me manners. So please, tell me the story."

Naomi chuckled at her tone and playful grin. "Sure. The story starts with my many times great-grandfather, August Bond, who came to this region in the late 1800s looking for gold. He had big plans and was going to get rich. Then he ended up meeting a lovely young native Sarcee maiden, Nukinu, who stole his heart. He fell in love and changed his plans. That was until she showed him the five gold nuggets her father had given her. He had warned her not to show any white person the gold or tell them where it came from because it would make them crazy. Make him leave to find the source. She didn't believe her father and trusted August. So she showed him the nuggets." Naomi paused, looking down at the necklace again.

"And what happened?"

"Well, August did go a bit crazy. Crazy with gold fever. But Nukinu wouldn't tell him where the gold came from. So he left to go find out for himself."

"Did he find gold? Did he get rich?"

Brittany's eager questions made Naomi laugh. "No, he didn't. Though not for lack of trying, apparently. He crossed the mountains, all the way digging and panning and trekking up rivers and streams. Then, according to the story, he was panning for gold, and he was cold and lonely and miserable and he thought of Nukinu."

"He missed her, didn't he?" Brittany interjected.

"Let Naomi finish the story," Jess said.

"Actually, yes, he did miss her. A lot. So he left his gold pans behind and went back to Nukinu and begged her to take him back. Thankfully, she did."

"I would have made him wait. Sweat it out," Brittany said, a curious edge to her voice. Naomi wondered if she was talking about the father of her baby.

"Well, luckily for me and my family, Nukinu was a forgiving sort of person and she took him back," Naomi continued. "August settled in the valley and started ranching."

"So the nuggets got passed down through the family?"

"They did. They were made into a bracelet that my nana Bond ended up wearing. Then, when my nana had a heart attack, she wanted all the kids to come home. She got the bracelet made into five necklaces. One for each of my sisters and for my cousins, Tanner and Garret. She gave them to us when we came back to Rockyview. She gave us a Bible, as well."

"Why a Bible?" Brittany asked.

Naomi fingered the necklace again, thinking of that moment she had with her grandmother when she gave Naomi the gifts. "She gave us the necklace to remind us of where we came from and gave us the Bible so we know where we're supposed to go."

"Are they all back now? Your cousins and sisters?"

"Shannon never left and, for the rest, yes, we're all back. I was the last one." Naomi thought back to that lonely time when she heard everyone was coming home but she didn't dare leave Billy, thinking he was dying soon. He'd hung on for another ten months.

"That's a cool story. And it's cool that you got a Bible, too. You have a Bible, too, don't you, Jess?"

Naomi couldn't help sending Jess a surprised look. He just shrugged but didn't answer the question.

Brittany giggled, then leaned closer to Naomi. "And he has a picture of a girl inside of it. I saw it. She has hair the same color as yours—a kind of reddish-blond."

"I don't think Naomi needs to hear—"

"I only saw it the one time. The girl is really pretty." Brittany reached over and punched Jess on the shoulder. "He won't tell me who it is, but he did tell me the girl was special."

Each word Brittany spoke created questions that amplified the emotions of the moment. Then Jess looked up and their gazes meshed. Held. She couldn't look away as a swarm of questions buzzed around her head.

"Can I see the picture again?" Brittany asked in a coy voice. "Maybe Naomi knows who it is."

"Did you have enough to eat?" Jess asked, giving Brittany a pointed look. "'Cause I'm thinking I should get back to work."

"Don't go," Brittany pleaded, clutching his arm as he moved

to stand up. "I won't tease you anymore." She glanced at Naomi, her expression apologetic. "I'm sorry. I know the girl in the picture is you."

Naomi felt her heart grow still. He still had her picture. In his Bible.

The two thoughts braided together creating an unexpected glow deep in her soul.

"I'm sorry," Brittany said, turning back to Jess. "Don't get mad at me. I still want to see the inside of the house."

"I'm sure Naomi has things she needs to do," Jess said, giving her an out.

But Naomi was curious herself to see what Jess had been so busy with the past few days.

"I wouldn't mind seeing the inside," Naomi said. "We have time."

"Okay, I can give you a mini-tour."

Naomi held his gaze and then Jess gave her the sudden gift of a smile, which slid past the defenses she'd spent the past few days building up against him.

"So I should carry her inside, then?" Jess asked, tipping a questioning eyebrow toward Brittany, seeking verification.

"Unfortunately, yes," Naomi said in return. "She shouldn't walk at all."

"We have to get you a wheelchair," Jess grunted, bending over to pick up Brittany.

"I ordered one through the hospital," Naomi said. "They said it wouldn't come for a couple of weeks yet."

"She might have her baby by then," Jess said, as he shouldered the door open and stepped inside. Naomi followed, dragging one of the chairs along for Brittany to sit on. The first thing Naomi noticed was the pervasive scent of paint. The second, how the butter-yellow walls captured the sun and seemed to amplify it.

"I sure hope it comes by then," Brittany grumbled. "I'm

getting tired of all this. Blood tests and eating on time and needles and all that stuff."

"It's for a good cause," Jess said, setting her in the chair. He straightened, then brushed a strand of hair away from her face and touched the tip of her nose with his forefinger. The motion created a curl of wistfulness deep in Naomi. He used to do that to her all the time, as well.

"You want a healthy baby, don't you?" Jess was asking Brittany.

"A baby." A glimmer of sorrow flitted over Brittany's face, as if the reality of the result of her pregnancy was only now making itself known. "Can't believe I'm having a baby. I don't know what I'm supposed to do with a baby." She pressed her lips together and Jess caught her by the shoulder and squeezed.

"You'll be fine," Jess said. "Just take it one step at a time."

"I wish Sheila was here," Brittany sighed.

A shadow of anger flitted over Jess's features but was replaced by a forced smile. "She said she might come next week. Closer to when the baby will be coming. You're in good hands now, so it'll be okay."

He sounded so calming, so soothing, his voice holding a note of authority that made even Naomi feel assured.

"So what do you think?" Jess asked, looking at Naomi.

Connor had glanced up when they came into the house, but was now crouched down beside what Naomi suspected was the island. The wood he had used was a deep, rich brown that contrasted with a lighter shade for the cabinet doors, giving it a unique, yet warm, effect.

But what drew her eye was at the end of the kitchen where, she suspected, the stove would be.

"It's beautiful," Brittany exclaimed as she looked around. "Love the kitchen cabinets. Love the color. And I like what you did with the stair railing."

Naomi turned her attention to where Brittany was pointing,

taking in the unique uprights on the stairs. They looked as if he had cut them from individual trees, then smoothed and varnished them.

"I did that myself," Jess said. "Took me longer than I thought it would, but I think it's worth it."

"Totally worth it," Brittany exclaimed, craning her neck to get a better look. Then a flash of light caught her attention. "Where did you get that bird thingy?" she asked, pointing to the sun catcher hanging in the living-room window.

"Found it in Jess's room," Connor put in, now leaning on the island he had just installed.

A flush warmed Naomi's cheeks as she glanced toward Connor. His deep brown eyes held hers a moment, a glint of humor in their depths, then he lifted his eyebrows. He knew she was the one who made it.

"Don't you have cabinets to shim or doors to adjust?" Jess asked, glowering at him.

"Taking a break." Connor seemed unfazed by Jess's exasperation. "Seeking inspiration from the presence of two beautiful ladies."

Jess simply rolled his eyes.

Brittany was still looking at the sun catcher, then she caught Jess's hand. "Hey, that sun catcher reminds me. Remember how you said you wanted to get stained-glass windows made for your office? You should totally do that with those four rectangle windows above these big ones."

Brittany pointed to a row of windows spanning the width of the large windows at the end of the living room. "Think how cool that would be."

"It would, but it's hard to find people to do that work," Jess said quietly. "It takes a special skill and you need to work with someone who would be willing to do the kind of picture or work you'd like."

Naomi felt her heart quicken as she looked at the windows,

wondering what a person would do with them. The four seasons, she thought. Water running past rocks and trees, using the striations of color in the glass to create the effect of flowing water. Various browns with just the right patterns for the rocks. A verdigris stain on the lead to give the idea of moss. A scene that would tie in with the rugged surroundings of this amazing house.

"Hey, Naomi, why are you smiling?" Brittany asked.

Naomi jerked her attention back, again feeling self-conscious as she met Jess's eyes. His expression was serious, as if he knew exactly what she was thinking.

"No reason," she said with a light laugh to cover her confusion. She made a show of looking at her watch. "We should probably let Jess get back to his work," she said to Brittany. "And we need to do another blood test and get you your insulin."

Brittany heaved out a sigh. "Okay, but can we come here again tomorrow?"

"Only if Jess—"

"As long as it's okay—"

Once again, Jess and Naomi spoke at the same time. A slow smile crawled across Jess's lips as he held up his fist and mouthed, *one, two, three.*

Naomi wanted to ignore him, but when he hit three, she mimed scissors just as he kept his hand in a fist.

"Guess I win," Jess murmured, tapping his fist against her hand.

"What's that about?" Brittany asked. "Why do you win?"

"I'll explain it another time," Jess said. "But Naomi's right. I better get back to work if I want to get this house done before winter."

He bent over, fitted his hands under Brittany's legs and lifted her up, then easily walked out the door, Naomi behind him.

Before she left the house, though, she glanced up at the bank of windows in the living room, trying to imagine how the light would look, diffused by the colored glass. Then, as she turned to leave, she caught Connor's knowing gaze.

"Would look really good," he said, as if he knew exactly what she was thinking. "I know Jess would love it."

She wanted to ignore his suggestion. What did it matter to her what Jess liked or didn't?

I want a place of light and peace.

Jess's words rang through her mind and for some reason she hadn't been able to forget the pain she saw in his eyes when he said it.

"I'm sure it would," was all Naomi said.

Then, with one last look around the house that was full of the light Jess wanted, she turned and left.

"You bringing your sister here again?" Connor asked as he screwed another hinge on the door.

Jess put down his carpenter's pouch and nodded. "Naomi said Brittany was in a much better mood after yesterday afternoon. So, yeah, I think so."

"I'm glad Naomi's back," Connor said. "She's good people."

Jess wasn't fooled by the pseudo-casual tone in Connor's voice. While he and Connor had always known each other, it wasn't until the past few years that they'd gotten close. But Rockyview wasn't big. Connor also knew Naomi and Jess had dated.

"That she is," Jess said. And too good for him.

"Why don't you ask her to make some windows for you?" Connor held up the door and fitted it to the frame. "Would make that living room look awesome. Wouldn't be surprised if she already has an idea of what to do."

"Why do you say that?"

"Because I saw her looking at the windows with a funny

smile, like she was imagining what they would look like all done up."

Jess waved off his comment and stifled the faint lift of hope Connor's words gave him. "Catch the rest of your act later," was all he said as he left the house.

He didn't need Connor giving him ideas he couldn't afford to indulge in. Naomi was only here to take care of Brittany. Once that job was done, she would be out of their lives.

Naomi stood by the counter putting sandwiches in a container when he came into the house. She wore her hair loose today, which was a pleasant surprise.

"Where's Brittany?" he asked.

"She's talking on the phone," Naomi said, biting her lip.

"You don't seem happy about that."

Naomi looked over her shoulder, as if making sure Brittany couldn't hear. "She's talking to Scott."

Jess frowned, not comprehending what Naomi was saying.

"The father of the baby," she added.

Jess felt ice slip through his veins and he clenched his hands at his side. "Really? *Now* he calls?"

"At least he called," Naomi said.

"I think I'd like to talk to that punk." Jess made a move toward the bedroom, but Naomi put her hand on his arm to stop him.

"Don't do that, please?" Naomi pleaded, her hazel eyes holding his.

Jess felt the anger slip away both at the sound of her voice and at her touch. He looked down at her slender fingers resting on his skin, warm and delicate, and he felt a quieting in his chest.

At the same time he had to fight the urge to cover her hand with his own.

She withdrew her hand slowly. Reluctantly?

Stop dreaming, Schroder. You're not the man for her.

So why is she looking at me like that?

He felt as if he was trying to keep a kite aloft in an ever-decreasing wind. It was becoming harder and harder to remind himself that she didn't belong with him. Every moment he spent with her made his heart believe that maybe it could happen, even when his mind told him otherwise.

"So...did he call her or did she call him?"

"He called her. I left the room when I knew."

Jess tore his attention away from Naomi and back to Brittany. "Has my mom called at all?"

Naomi shook her head. "No, she hasn't."

Jess blew out a ragged sigh, then turned back to Naomi. "I shouldn't be surprised. Mom never seemed to get the idea of how motherhood worked."

Naomi tilted her head to one side, a tiny dent of uncertainty marring her face. "Was it that bad?"

"Define bad."

"My own mother wasn't the best mother," Naomi said quietly, leaning back against the counter. "She still isn't. I got a card from her when Billy died, but she hasn't called me since. But I recognize she's had a hard life and I'm willing to forgive her for that. My father left her with three children to take care of. She did the best she could with what she was given. I wouldn't say she was a great mother. I hope to make better choices than she did when the time comes, but at the same time, I hope I don't have to deal with what she did."

Jess looked at her, surprised at her capacity to forgive. So why couldn't she seem to forgive him?

Did it matter? They were both in different places in their lives. Her forgiveness, or lack thereof, had no bearing on where he or she was right now.

"My mother has made her own choices, as well. Most of them pretty lousy." He caught himself. He was starting to sound like he felt sorry for himself. "How long has she been talking to that Scott kid?" he asked, changing the subject.

"About half an hour now."

"She'll probably be done soon. I can wait," Jess said, hiding behind his stepsister's wishes as an excuse to stay.

"Okay."

It was thickly quiet for a moment in that awkward way that made him want to blurt out something, anything to fill the silence.

"So how hard is it to make a stained-glass window?" he asked, shooting out the first thing that came to his mind. "I mean, if I wanted someone to do some like Brittany was talking about."

"It would depend on how complicated you wanted it to be."

Jess nodded, shifting his weight. "So what would you do? If you had to make those windows?"

He didn't miss the light of expectation flickering in her eyes. She had thought about it just as Connor had said.

"I would suggest to someone who was making them to think about the things you like. To incorporate something from the surrounding area, colors, flow, water, trees, that kind of thing." Her hands made shapes as if envisioning how the windows would look.

"So what would *you* do?" he asked, pulling the conversation back to her, pleased at the happiness in her voice and the light in her eyes.

"The four seasons of a creek. It would start with winter, snowdrifts and at the far end of the first window a flash of water. Then it would flow through spring and summer and fall, each window showing the creek moving but each window displaying a different season. You have rocks with moss and trees alongside, flashes of light and sparkles of water that could be done with small jewels." Her smile grew as her voice rose and her enthusiasm created a Naomi-shaped space in his heart.

Since she had come here, he hadn't seen her this animated. This was the girl he remembered. This bright-eyed person, excited and full of life. "Would you be willing to make them?" he asked before thought or reason could interfere.

She stopped suddenly, her hands still hovering in the air. Then she slowly lowered them, her eyes following her hands. She looked like she was deflating and his heart followed. Then she slowly shook her head. "I'm not sure. I don't think I can," was all she said. She looked up at him, holding his eyes. "I don't think I should." Then she looked down. "I think I'll have lunch by myself today."

Then, in what seemed to be a steady refrain in their lives, she turned and walked away from him.

CHAPTER 7

"I don't think you should do it," Hailey said as Naomi set her purse on the floor under the pew. All around them people filed into church, chatting and laughing; and woven through all that was worship music coming from the speakers situated in the corners of the church sanctuary.

"I know. Working on the windows would mean working even more closely with Jess."

"You have to work with him enough. You're smart to try to keep your distance."

Naomi abruptly shoved the bulletin in front of the Bible in the rack in front of her. Jess represented a time of her life that had taken her over. Consumed her. Being around him too much only served to bring all that back. She had never told her sisters about her and Jess being together intimately and the longer she had kept that secret, the more difficult it became to release.

Being around Jess created a storm of emotions that rose from the past. Guilt. Shame.

"So how are the wedding plans coming?" Naomi asked, abruptly shifting the topic. Jess occupied enough time in her thoughts and lately was confusing her more and more.

"Coming along," Hailey said. "Did you have a chance to check out that website for dresses?"

"I picked up my laptop from the apartment. The internet at Jess's is spotty but I'll try to check it out this afternoon."

"Let me know which ones you like." Hailey plucked the mutilated bulletin from the pew rack and scanned it herself. "If you don't find anything on the site, I was hoping we could run up to Calgary and have a look at a couple of bridal stores there."

There was a wonderful store in Calgary that stocked stained-glass supplies.

Naomi caught herself, giving her head a mental shake. Thankfully the worship team had come to the front and she joined in the singing, letting herself be immersed in worship. Since taking care of Brittany, she hadn't been in church much.

"You knew us, Lord, before we gave breath, You wove us in our mother's womb. You hold our lives, in the palms of Your hands, You guide us, Lord, from life to tomb."

The words of the song Faith Tye sang seeped into her own soul. Brought up memories she had struggled with for years to erase. She closed her eyes, imagining God holding her life in the palms of his hands. Holding the child she had carried for such a brief moment in her own womb.

She fought down a slow sob, surprised that after all this time the memory came seeping back and behind it the shame she had hid all these years but had slowly started creeping around the edges of her mind of late.

It was being here with Jess so close by. Being back in Rockyview that enticed the memories back and with it the shame she had fought so long.

She and Jess had been so caught up in each other. So young and careless; overcome with passion and large, grand emotions that, in the end, had burned them both up.

You were the only one.

Her impulsive words came back, echoing in her mind.

He was the only one. And because of that act, she had gotten pregnant. Then, three months later, after her regret and shame sent her back to Billy, after Jess had locked her out of his life, had told her he could never be a father, she had lost his child.

"Are you okay?" Hailey asked, whispering as she touched Naomi's arm.

Naomi gave a tight nod, then turned her attention back to the pastor. He spoke of God's forgiveness and how unconditional it was and Naomi clung to that comfort. She knew she was forgiven, yet the memory of that moment of weakness still lingered and created the sorrow she was now struggling with.

That's because of what happened. Because of the pregnancy.

Naomi pushed the accusing voice aside. Then the minister invited everyone to pray, and as Naomi closed her eyes, she opened her soul to God.

Help me, Lord, to put the past behind me, she prayed. *Help me to know what I should do about Jess.*

She felt as if things were shifting between them, and she was trying to catch her balance in this new place. Trying to keep her hand on her own identity. Trying to keep the past where it belonged. But being around Jess kept creating cracks in her self-imposed defense.

Thankfully Hailey said nothing to her as they got up to sing the last song and then turned to leave, joining the people slowly meandering down the aisle to the back of the church.

"So are you going to Nana's for lunch before you go to the inn?" Naomi asked her sister, trying to find her normal again.

"Nana, Tanner, Sabine, and Olivia are driving across the valley to visit an old friend of Nana's. And Shannon and I are going up to the inn to talk to Garret and Larissa about what we're doing there for the wedding. Do you want to come?"

Naomi shook her head. Much as she loved being involved with her sister's double wedding plans, being around three engaged family members—Shannon, Hailey, and her cousin

Garret—was a bit overwhelming. Besides, it reminded her too much about her own eternal engagement to Billy.

An engagement that, in her mind, had been in name only. She had wanted to break up with him and had even chosen the day it would happen. The same day he was diagnosed with cancer. Naomi had known she couldn't do that to him, so she stayed with him until the end. She never regretted her decision, but it had taken its toll on her emotions and her life.

"I'm fine," she said waving off Hailey's invitation. "I should get back to Brittany anyway."

"If you change your mind, you know where we'll be."

Naomi nodded, then made her way outside. When she reached her car, she heard a voice calling her name.

She turned around to see an unfamiliar young man loping toward her. He was tall, thin, with a shock of black hair and dark eyes that seemed to dominate his narrow face. His denim jacket was torn at the sleeves and his blue jeans had seen better days.

"Are you Naomi Deacon?" he asked as he came to a stop in front of her.

She nodded. "Yes, I am. And you might be?"

The young man shoved his hands in his pockets, awkwardly shifting from foot to foot. "You, uh, don't know me. I, uh, came to the church 'cause the guy at the gas station told me you'd probably be here and some lady in church told me who you were."

"And your name is...?" she prompted.

"Sorry. Yeah. Sorry." He scratched the side of his face, and shifted his feet again. "My name is Scott and Brittany tells me that you're the one taking care of her. She told me. Last time I talked to her."

Scott. The father of Brittany's baby.

Anger seared a path down her spine as she straightened. She

wanted to say a hundred things to him but knew none would be helpful.

Besides, she had just come out of church, had just been reminded of her own past transgressions, so she tempered her thoughts and went with the straightforward facts.

"She misses you," Naomi said. "She's scared."

Scott looked down at the ground, his foot scuffing the gravel of the parking lot. "Yeah. Well, I kind of miss her, too. I'm scared, too."

His reluctant confession ignited a ray of hope. "So what are you doing about that?"

Scott's only reply was a heavy sigh, then he reached in his jacket pocket and pulled out a wrinkled envelope that looked like it had traveled many miles. "Could you give that to her?"

Naomi took the envelope, lifting her eyebrows in a questioning look.

"It's some money. For the baby. And a letter for her."

"Why don't you come with me? You could deliver it yourself," Naomi suggested.

Scott lifted his hands as if pushing her and her suggestion away. "No can do. Not yet. I'm not ready to be a dad yet."

What was it with men and fatherhood? What were they so afraid of?

Naomi tucked the envelope in her purse, holding his dark gaze.

"She's all alone, you know. Her stepmother isn't even around."

"Yeah, but she has her brother."

Naomi felt her heart knock at her ribs at the idea of Jess helping Brittany with her baby. Jess had made it fairly clear that being any kind of father figure in this child's life wasn't happening. So how will that work?

"You're this baby's father." She kept her tone as gentle and nonthreatening as possible considering that part of her wanted to shake some sense and responsibility into him.

"I know. I know. But right now..." He clenched his fists. "Just say hey to her. Tell her...tell her that...never mind." Then he spun around and loped down the parking lot toward a large truck that had some kind of metal box on the back. Looked like a welding truck. He started it up and then, with a growl, he burned out of the parking lot.

Naomi watched him go, emotions flashing through her. Anger. Concern. Sorrow. But stitched through them all was a slender thread of pity for a young, confused boy.

She turned away, her own burden still resting heavily on her shoulders.

Jess knocked lightly on the bedroom door and when Brittany invited him in, he opened it. Brittany lay on the bed, paging through a glossy magazine.

"Lunch is ready," he said.

"Is Naomi back from church yet?" she asked, looking up from her magazine.

"I don't figure on her coming back for a few hours." He had made the offer for Naomi to take the day off, knowing that she probably wanted to go to church as well as connect with her family.

He bent over and lifted Brittany up. "So do you want to eat on the deck of my house or sit in the kitchen?"

"Kitchen is fine."

"Don't sound so enthusiastic," he said as he made his way down the hallway. She was getting heavier and he didn't know how much longer he would be able to pack her around.

For a moment he wondered what would happen after the

baby was born. Panic slivered through him but he caught himself.

He had to get hold of his mother. Make her own up to her responsibilities.

If she doesn't?

He couldn't go there. He had to trust she'd do the right thing.

"Is that all you're eating?" Jess asked when he was done his lunch. Brittany had only nibbled on her sandwich, barely touched the soup Naomi had made, and had one of the strawberries sitting in a bowl beside her. "Naomi said you have to make sure to eat everything or you'll have an insulin reaction again."

"I'm not hungry," she said in a choked voice as she pushed her plate away and he took it, wondering what to do. He set it on the counter, and when he returned, she was looking away, her lips pressed together, her hair hiding her face.

Jess knelt down beside her, resting his forearms on the arm of the easy chair. "What's wrong, Brit?"

Her only reply was a sniff.

Oh, great. Was she crying? What was he supposed to do about that?

"Aw, honey, don't cry. It's okay. Things will work out."

And then she started hiccupping, choking out deep, wrenching sobs.

Good job on the comforting, Jess thought. He was obviously not cut out for this kind of thing.

"I don't think they will," she cried. "I talked to Scott. He's...he's..."

"Scott is a louse. He should either step up to his responsibilities or leave you alone."

"I am alone. All alone," she cried, plunging her face into her hands. Her shoulders shook and Jess felt completely and utterly helpless.

Her sobs tore at his heart and he knelt there a while, wishing he could take away her pain. Finally he couldn't stand it anymore.

"Brit, it's okay," he said, needing to say something. Anything. "If you need a place after the baby is born...you can...you can stay here." He felt as if he had to drag the words out one by one and he knew his heart wasn't in the offer, but what else could he do? His mother wasn't stepping up and the boyfriend was AWOL. Who else would help the girl? He wasn't any kind of father figure, but what else could he do?

The back door opened and Naomi stood in the doorway, her hazel eyes looking from him to Brittany and back again, her face holding a curious expression.

And to his dismay, the unexpected sight of her sent his own heart into overdrive.

He turned back to Brittany. "Naomi's here, sweetie," he said, touching her shoulder.

Brittany choked back the next sob, then lifted her face, palming her tears off her cheeks. She gave Naomi a wavery smile. "You're back."

"Is everything okay?"

"Jess made me lunch," Brittany said, her voice thick with unshed tears. "And I'm feeling rotten. I couldn't eat."

Jess got to his feet, feeling suddenly self-conscious. "She's upset."

Naomi knelt down beside her and stroked her hair. "What's wrong?"

"Scott. He called me. I asked if he was coming, but he said no." Brittany heaved a sigh. "I have a headache and I'm tired. I want to go to bed."

"Sure. Of course." Naomi got up and looked over at the half finished sandwich. "You sure you can't eat any more?"

Brittany shook her head.

"Okay. I'll adjust your insulin." Naomi glanced over at Jess and he came and lifted Brittany out of the chair.

He brought her back to the bed and then left.

While Naomi settled Brittany, he cleaned up the kitchen, wondering again what had gotten into him when he offered to let Brittany stay with him.

Was he crazy? He didn't know the first thing about kids. Or babies. He was no good at that kind of thing.

He felt an all-too-familiar fear rise from his stomach. What if...

He closed his eyes, gripping the edges of the plate. *Please, Lord, help me through this. Help me to do the right thing. Give me the strength to do the right thing.*

Because he knew there was no way he could do this on his own. Not with his legacy.

"I think she'll sleep for a while." Naomi's quiet voice broke into his thoughts.

Jess nodded and finished up, then wiped his hands down the sides of his pants. "So if you're okay here—"

This time he would be the one to leave.

"Actually, I need to talk to you." She sounded serious. "It's about Scott," she said, her voice quiet. She glanced back down the hall, as if concerned Brittany might hear.

"Okay, tell me," he said as he sat down at the table, resting his elbows on its scarred surface. The table had come with the house and still bore the initials of whoever had lived here before. A family with brothers and sisters and parents who stuck around. That much he knew. Sometimes, before Brittany came, he would sit in the living room trying to imagine what kind of family gatherings took place there. And now, here he was. With a sixteen-year-old stepsister down the hall expecting a baby. Some kind of family this was.

"Tell me about Scott." He couldn't stop the note of anger from entering his voice.

"I saw him at church this morning."

"Church?" Jess sat up, his hands turning into fists. "What was he doing there? Why didn't he come here? Brittany is tearing up inside because it seems he doesn't want to step up to his responsibilities."

Naomi held her hand up, making a shushing noise. "Keep your voice down. I don't want Brittany to hear," she whispered.

"So what did that louse have to say?"

Naomi reached down and pulled an envelope out of her purse. She laid it on the table. "He didn't say much, but he gave me this. Said it was money for Brittany and a letter."

"Really? That's the best he could do?" Jess pushed the envelope away with one finger, as if he didn't want to come into contact with it.

Naomi sat back in her chair, her arms folded over the white ruffly shirt she wore. "I know it isn't what we hoped for, but it's a start."

"It's nothing."

Naomi tapped her fingers on her arm, rocking lightly in her chair as if thinking. "You are a bundle of contradictions, aren't you?"

Jess was taken aback at her quiet comment. "What do you mean?"

"You expect Scott to step up and take care of his responsibilities, be a father to this baby, and yet you've always said you couldn't be a father yourself."

"I can't."

"Can't or won't?"

He waved off her question. "Why are we talking about me? We're supposed to be talking about Scott."

"And you've offered Brittany a place to stay. With you."

Jess frowned at her, trying to follow her line of reasoning. "Well, yeah, the kid needs a place."

Then, to his surprise, Naomi gave him a gentle smile. "That's generous and caring of you. You're a good man, Jess Schroder. Better than you think."

Her praise settled on his soul and he felt a quieting in his spirit. He held her gaze for another beat and again he felt a rising of emotions he hadn't felt in a long while.

Attraction.

Connection.

Peace.

Naomi was the only one who could make him feel peaceful even though the past few days of being around her made him feel anything but.

He wanted to look away but couldn't. Wanted to touch her but shouldn't. "Thanks for that," he muttered. "I feel like I'm at a complete loss here."

"Of course you are. I think parents always are. My mom used to tell me it would have been so much easier if we came with instruction manuals. She said parenting was like trying to build a boat while you're out at sea. You're always just trying to catch up." She eased out a gentle smile. "I sometimes wished she was a better mother, but I think she did the best she could with what she was given. Besides, we had our nana and papa who gave us all the love and caring we ever needed." She looked over at Jess. "You don't have to be a father to this baby. Being a brother to Brittany is already honorable. Like I said, I think you sell yourself short. Offering to take Brittany in and help support her is one of the most generous things I've ever seen."

"More generous than anything Billy would have done?" As soon as the words spilled out, Jess mentally slapped his forehead. Why had he brought up Billy? Was he deliberately trying to sabotage this moment?

Naomi's smile shifted, but only a bit. "Billy was a generous person, but his generosity came with...conditions."

He knew he shouldn't ask, but the way she had said that hinted that things had not been so rosy between her and Billy. And he felt a tiny ray of hope.

"Conditions like what?"

Naomi tore her gaze away and for a moment he wondered if she would say anything.

"I'm sorry, it's none of my business. It's just, you seldom talk about Billy."

"It's fine. I don't mind." But she was quiet a moment again.

So he said nothing, giving her space.

"When Billy and I...got together again, we moved to British Columbia and went to college there," she said finally, releasing a melancholy smile. "I was enrolled in an art course. I wanted to do more with my stained-glass work. Billy took his divinity courses and then, when he proposed, suggested, in a way that I couldn't refuse, that I take something that would work better with his degree. He still had thoughts of going into the mission field and said that an art course wouldn't translate into anything that would be acceptable on the field. So he persuaded me to switch my courses and take a nursing degree with an eye to what would work for him. I didn't want to spend that much time and money and instead I took a nurse's aide course. It made sense. Art and mission work don't work together very well." She gave a short laugh. "I guess I had always hoped I could go back and finish my art degree later."

She went quiet then and looked down at her hands, as if she felt she had betrayed Billy's memory and said too much.

For Jess, however, it was a glimpse into what her life with Billy had been and gave him a faint notion that maybe Billy had not been quite the perfect man for her. Not if he couldn't see what she had done with glass. How she changed the light with her work, enhanced it. Made it sing.

If Billy couldn't see that, did he know who she truly was?

"Did you ever do any stained-glass work after that?"

Naomi slowly shook her head, twisting the button on her sweater as she spoke. "I didn't have time once I switched my courses. And it was hard...hard to find money to pay for supplies and a reason to do it."

Jess remembered watching Naomi work on the sun catcher she had made for him. She had had a makeshift studio set up in her bedroom and in one corner, she had a small lamp she had made for somebody and another one for her grandmother.

"I remember how excited you were when Baxter Lincoln asked you to make a window for his house."

Naomi's smile grew melancholy. "I remember thinking that was my big break. But I also remember feeling like I needed to know more about color and light and composition and flow." She gave a light laugh. "I had no clue."

"And now?"

"I ended up taking some courses in Halifax the last year of his life. Billy was sick so much of the time and couldn't do his work. I learned so much. It was wonderful." Her smile grew, she sat straighter and her eyes lit up as if they were windows themselves. Windows into her soul. "I learned how to use color. How to paint on glass. How to make glass. We were going to do this tour of some of the cathedrals in Quebec City, but I couldn't..." Her voice trailed off and Jess suspected her switching of majors had much to do with the aborted trip.

Then she turned to him, her smile wavering, as if unsure. "I know I said I didn't want to do the windows for your house, but if the offer is still open..."

Jess held her hesitant gaze, then nodded. "I would love it if you could do them."

Her smile settled into his being. And as their gazes held, Jess felt the old connection. The old emotions. And yet, behind them, something deeper. Stronger.

Something that had the potential to upset every aspect of his life.

CHAPTER 8

"So I thought I would use this brown down in this corner and slowly work toward a striated green here." Naomi pointed with her pencil to the sketches she had spent most of the afternoon drawing up.

She had been working at the kitchen table when Jess had come in the house, ostensibly to get something from his room. When she invited him to look at the sketches she was making for his window, he had readily agreed.

Now he stood beside her, so close she could smell the scent of sawdust and beneath that a hint of the brand of soap she remembered he always used.

The soap she had given him as a gift.

Her heart clenched, then she pushed off the reaction, turning her focus back to the sketches she had made.

"I thought I would work with each window representing a season of the year," she said, pointing to the pictures with her pencil. "The first window would be of an ice-covered creek which would be melting in the second window, then clear in the third window to represent summer and in the last one, a few brown leaves floating in the water with a hint of white on the far side to bring it full circle to the beginning. The trees and shrubs on the banks of the creek would each show the changing seasons, as well."

"Sounds perfect," Jess said, his voice a quiet rumble. "Are you using lead or copper foil?" He leaned closer, his hands resting on the table. She saw a jagged scar across the back of one hand that he got when they had gone mountain biking. He had taken a run too fast, had fallen and cut his hand open. He had laughed, ripped the sleeve off his T-shirt and used it as a makeshift bandage, insisting on biking the rest of the way down the hill.

Always tough as nails. He would never say he couldn't do something. And he always pushed her, as well. Pushed her beyond her comfort zone, pushed her to try things she never would have on her own. Around him she had always felt a bit frightened as well as energized and enervated.

She blinked, pulling herself back from the brink of the old memories that came more frequently the more time she spent around Jess. Maybe she shouldn't have taken on this project. Was she crazy?

In spite of her questioning thoughts, she was glad for the job. When she had started sketching out the design, she felt suddenly whole and alive. Something she hadn't felt...

Since Jess.

"I was thinking lead," she said hastily, scribbling a note in the margin as she pulled herself back to the moment. "The windows will be too heavy for foil and lead will be more forgiving. It's been years since I cut glass and I don't trust my accuracy anymore."

"Do you know where you're getting the glass?"

"Hailey said she was going to Calgary to look at bridesmaid dresses. There's a store there that carries all the supplies I need."

"I can take care of Brittany when you go."

"You don't need to worry about that. Shannon said she would come to watch Brittany. Though she's been much more cooperative lately. I even got her doing her own blood tests yesterday."

Jess nodded, a slow smile creeping across his lips. "You've done good work with her," he said quietly. "I can't tell you how much I appreciate your help and support. Having you around has been a real blessing."

His praise warmed her soul and his steady gaze holding hers slowed her heart.

A finger of fear tugged at her thoughts as she found herself unable to pull her gaze away from him.

Don't lose yourself again. Don't get taken over. Stay in charge of your emotions and your life.

Then, when his hand came up to brush a strand of hair away from her face, the touch of his fingers tracing her cheek on her face made a mockery of her struggle to maintain her distance.

Look away. Look away.

But her protests faded as their gazes meshed, held, and time slowly wheeled around them. Her heart quickened and again she felt as if she was a young girl amazed that this incredibly handsome man wanted anything to do with her.

Then he dragged his eyes away, breaking the connection, and behind the feeling of relief came a sense of loss.

He could always do that to her, Naomi reminded herself as she turned her attention back to the sketches. Always make her feel as if he was the only person in the world.

Then, when he retreated, make you feel all alone.

The words created a cold clarity. She had made the same mistake with Billy. Losing herself so completely in his life and his personality that she had lost any sense of her own wants and needs.

Yet, she knew that with Jess it was all different. She felt alive around Jess. She felt whole.

"I'm impressed," Jess said, straightening, his voice gruff,

which made her wonder if he was as affected as she was. "You've got some original and wonderful ideas."

She swallowed and took a deep breath to center herself.

"Thank you," she said quietly, her heart and mind slowly coming back to earth. "I just hope they translate to wonderful windows."

Her nerves fluttered at the thought of working with glass again. Of trying to express her vision using a brittle and unforgiving medium. "I'm pretty rusty."

"I'm sure you'll do great. You don't settle for mediocre," he said, giving her another quick smile.

She felt as if his words held a deeper meaning.

"I'll do my best," she said, affecting a breezy tone. "After all, you're paying my wages. I'm just the help."

Jess's expression darkened. "You're more than that." His voice held a peculiar tone that Naomi wasn't sure she wanted to think about. Not with her own emotions so tenuous right now. Yet, she couldn't look away from him, and worse, didn't want to.

Then, when Jess's hand came up and his fingers rested feather-light on her cheek, she heard a warning knell sound in her soul.

Danger. Danger.

But the old yearning Jess could always evoke in her, the heart-wrenching loneliness that had been her companion those long years after Jess, rose, quenching the reprimand.

She felt herself leaning toward him as the air around them amplified and filled with light.

Then, loneliness and an old forgotten ache made her turn her face into his hand. Made her reach up to encircle his wrist with her fingers.

She closed her eyes as if to shut out everything else. To focus only on the roughness of Jess's fingers. The warmth of his hand on her face.

She had missed him. So badly she had missed him.

She felt a beat of disloyalty to Billy and she tried to bring up her fiancé's face. To remind herself of what Billy had done for her.

Then Jess's fingers tightened, Billy faded away and for a heart-stopping moment she thought Jess might kiss her.

Instead Jess withdrew his hand and Naomi felt bereft.

She turned away, suddenly ashamed of how easily she had forgotten. How quickly she allowed herself to get pulled into the force of Jess's personality.

And how easily she forgot Billy and what he had done for her.

"I better go," Jess said quietly.

She nodded, not sure what she should do. Then, to her surprise and dismay, he bent over and brushed his lips over her cheek. "Good night, Naomi," he said quietly.

Then he left her to her swirling thoughts and confused emotions, her heart beating in her neck, her soul both distraught and lonely.

She sank down into the chair behind her and pressed her hands together, lowering her head.

Lord, help me through this. I need to keep my feet on solid ground. You are my solid ground. You are my only true identity.

She took a slow breath, willing her pounding heart to still. Glancing sidelong, she saw the sketches she had been making for Jess's window.

One step at a time, she reminded herself. *Don't go jumping into anything. You're just doing a job for him. Don't get distracted by old emotions and feelings that, at one time, took over your entire life.*

Even as these words rang through her mind like a litany of self-control, behind them crept a sense of rightness. Of completion that she had never felt with Billy.

She looked down at the sketches again, a mixture of anticipation and nervousness pulsing through her. She would be working with glass again and making something beautiful that would come alive when the light shone through it.

She would be making windows for Jess Schroder's house.

Trouble was, she wasn't sure which idea made her feel the most alive.

"So tell me why you've been putzing away at this house for the past four years and now, all of a sudden, you're putting the screws on us to get this done?" Connor screwed a handle onto another cabinet door, tightening it with a grunt.

Jess pulled out a handle for the last cabinet door out of the box sitting on the granite countertop and brushed the dust off. "Just tired of having it sit here, half finished. Besides, I'll probably need the space for Brittany if she needs to stay."

"That's pretty big of you. Taking in a girl you're not even technically related to."

Jess shrugged off Connor's comment. He didn't feel like it was pretty big of him. In fact, there were many times he felt like chasing down Brittany's ex-boyfriend and having a few words with him.

"Elliot Tye and I have a bet going that you're going after Naomi again."

Again. The word sounded pathetic in Jess's ears. Even as he let the idea settle, he felt as if he wasn't going back in time. Naomi had changed a lot since she had left Rockyview. She had a maturity, a quiet resilience about her that, if anything, made her more attractive to him than before.

"Well, you better cancel the bet," Jess said, holding out the handle. "That's the last of 'em."

Connor held Jess's gaze. "You never got over her, did you?"

Jess wanted to ignore his friend's comment or, better yet,

brush him off with a joke, but then Connor leaned his large arms on the counter, as if settling in for a chat.

"You've always liked her," Connor said. "Even when you were dating other girls, I know she's always been the one for you."

"You sound like a junior high schoolgirl." Jess dropped the handle on the counter with a clunk, a not-so-subtle hint to keep working.

"So what's holding you back?" Connor asked, ignoring Jess's remark and the handle. "I see how she looks at you. I'm sure she still thinks about you."

Jess folded his arms over his chest, Connor's words igniting a tiny spark of hope deep within. Yesterday, after he had left Naomi, he had felt like smacking himself on the head any number of times for the impulsive kiss he had given her. It was as if he couldn't help himself.

He hadn't stuck around to catch her reaction either.

This morning he had stayed away from the house, but lunchtime was quickly approaching and he would have to face Naomi again.

"Doesn't matter what you're sure of. She's just buried her fiancé. A guy who was studying to be a minister. I'm not anywhere in his league."

Connor's eyes narrowed. "Why do you think that? You're ten times the man Billy Phelan ever was."

Billy had never taken advantage of Naomi the way Jess had.

But Jess couldn't say those words aloud. What had happened between him and Naomi was something that had affected him on so many levels. Even though he was ashamed, at the same time it had created a connection between him and Naomi that he had never shared with any other woman he had dated since.

You were the only one.

"I'm not anything like Billy," Jess said, pushing the handle toward Connor. "He's the guy who's marriage and father material."

But still Connor stood across from him.

"Maybe. Billy was an okay guy, but I can't see him doing for Brittany what you're doing without any strings attached. You've shown her love and caring and I've never heard you make her feel like she was less of a person for what happened to her."

"How could I?" Jess asked. "I'm not a better person than her."

Connor straightened, resting his hands on the countertop. "That's what makes you better than Billy. I doubt he would have said the same thing. And that's why I think you're a way better man than he was. Naomi would be lucky to have a guy like you in her life," Connor said quietly.

Jess waved off his comment. "Thanks for the pep talk, but I've got too much stuff that comes attached."

Connor didn't say anything to that. Instead he picked up the handle and Jess thought the conversation was finally done. But then Connor heaved out a heavy sigh, hefting the handle from one hand to other, seeming to weigh his words. "You don't still believe all that garbage your old man tossed at you, do you? The things he used to say to you?"

Jess pulled his hand over his face, as if erasing those words of derision from his father that could, at times, pull him down to where his father seemed to want him.

"I know God is my heavenly Father and He loves me unconditionally," Jess said, raising his head. "But when your earthly father has told you you're worthless for most of your life, when all you've ever heard from him is that he wished you were never born, it takes time and miles to move past that."

Connor nodded in understanding. He was the only friend of Jess's who knew exactly what he'd had to deal with. Connor was the only one Jess had confided in.

He hadn't seen it all, though.

Then a light tap at the door broke into the heavy silence and

Jess turned to see Naomi standing in the doorway, the light haloing her hair and casting her features in shadow.

She cleared her throat, then held up Jess's cell phone. "I'm sorry to bother you, but your mother called and I took the liberty of answering. She said she needed to talk to you."

Jess blinked, trying to get his bearings, wondering what Naomi might have overheard.

"Is she still on the phone?"

"No. She hung up before I could get here."

"I'll call her back later," he said, walking over to take the phone from Naomi. "Sorry about that."

As she handed him the phone, she gave him a sudden smile that was like a gift. As if what happened yesterday was okay with her.

He returned it and the light in her eyes kindled emotions only Naomi had been able to create in him. Warmth. Caring. Belonging.

"Are you coming to bring Brittany over for lunch?" she asked, her voice lowering, drawing him closer to her.

"Yes, if you still figure on it."

"Of course."

Their words were inconsequential chitchat, but for Jess their very ordinariness affirmed what happened between them last night. As if Naomi was accepting them and was willing to make the shift into this new place they were, even now, exploring as their gazes held.

"Give me another half hour and I'll be there."

She gave him another smile, then left.

Without even turning around Jess could feel Connor's grin. He chose to ignore it and instead picked up another box of handles and knobs. "I'll put these on the bathroom cabinets," was all he said to Connor.

"Don't be messing up my handiwork," was all Connor said with a huge grin.

Jess just nodded. As he clomped up the stairs, he let himself smile and allow a glimmer of hope and optimism into his day.

He quickly got the handles attached and even though he told Naomi half an hour, twenty minutes later he was at the house.

Naomi was washing dishes in the sink, chatting with Brittany who lay in the old recliner they had pulled into the kitchen.

"What are you working on, Brit?" he asked, walking to her side, still fully aware of Naomi working at the counter.

"Naomi taught me how to knit and I'm trying to make a sweater." Brittany held up what she was doing. "Does it look okay?"

"Looks great," he said, hoping he put the right amount of admiration into his voice, considering he had no clue what he was looking at.

"Naomi's sister Shannon brought some wool from Naomi's nana here this morning. She'll be taking care of me when Naomi goes to get your glass tomorrow." Brittany held the knitted square out in front of her, turning it this way and that.

"It looks small for a sweater," Jess said.

"That's 'cause babies are small," Brittany returned with a grin.

Really small. He couldn't help the panic that clenched his stomach at the thought of a tiny baby wearing that tiny sweater.

One thing at a time. Jess touched her shoulder, then he turned to Naomi, who was watching him and Brittany. When their eyes met, a light flush pinkened her cheeks.

"I'm not quite ready," Naomi said.

"That's okay. I got done quicker than I thought," Jess said. "Sure smells good in here."

"Thought I would try something different, so I made burritos. I made enough so that Connor can have some, too, if he wants."

"He'll love you forever. He's crazy about burritos."

This netted him another quick smile, broader than the

first. Again their gazes meshed and again he couldn't look away as he recognized the first delicate steps in a fragile dance.

But she seemed willing to follow and if that was the case, he was willing to lead. So he took a step closer and gently brushed a soap bubble from her cheek and let his hand linger.

She turned her head, just a fraction, as if to maintain the contact.

"I think I made a mistake," Brittany called out.

Naomi pulled back and Jess lowered his hand.

As Naomi bent over Brittany, he leaned his hips back against the counter, his attention more on Naomi than his stepsister.

As he watched her help Brittany, a prayer drifted into his mind.

Dear Lord, help me to figure out where we are going and what we are doing.

But even as he released the words of his prayer, even as Naomi glanced his way, her smile growing, the old poison crept into his mind.

You're not worthy. You're not wanted. You're nothing like Billy.

He shook them off, but remnants of those accusations clung like dirt. Would he ever be completely free of them?

His phone rang and he quickly grabbed it, glancing at the call display before he answered. His mother.

"Hey, Mom. Sorry I didn't return your call," he said as he walked into the living room. "How are you doing?"

"I'm okay. I feel like things are coming together." This was followed by a dramatic sigh. "How is Brittany? Still on bed rest?"

"Yes. Naomi is taking her to the doctor in a couple of days to see how things are progressing, but so far her blood sugars are stabilized and her blood pressure is acceptable."

"That's good to know." Another moment of silence. "How is the house coming?"

"Connor is putting the cabinets in right now and the

plumber is coming again to install the sinks and showerheads. It will be ready in a couple of days, as well."

"That was quick. Considering it took you so many years to get it this far."

Jess said nothing to that. He had been pulling a few all-nighters to get things done. Lately he felt an unspoken urgency to get his house finished and ready.

For Naomi?

He pushed the question aside. He couldn't let himself indulge in that fantasy.

"So what can I do for you, Mom?" He moved farther away from the kitchen door and lowered his voice. "Are you coming back here anytime soon?"

Another moment of silence. "I believe I will. I know I have to. I just don't know...don't know if I'm ready to deal with her and a baby."

"Please think about it, Mom. You're the only mother she has and she'll need you once that baby comes."

"I know." This was followed by another heavy sigh. "I'm calling for another reason, though. I'm thinking of selling our house in Rockyview and I thought I should talk to you about it first."

"It's your house, too, Mom."

"You grew up there. It's where you spent your childhood and teen years. I assumed you would want to be informed."

Jess released a bitter laugh thinking of what those childhood and teen years entailed. Long lonely nights spent with a variety of nannies and housekeepers. And when his parents were home...

"It doesn't matter to me what you do with the house. I'm building my own place." And creating my own memories.

"Okay. I just needed to know so I can inform the renters. As for Brittany...I will come. I'm just not sure when."

He knew he couldn't expect more than this from his mother.

So he bade her a quiet goodbye and then ended the call. He closed his eyes, releasing a heavy sigh, hoping his mother would realize what her responsibilities were.

He felt a clutch of panic at the thought of the outcome of Brittany's pregnancy. A baby. Helpless and dependent.

Just then he heard Naomi's quiet murmur as she helped Brittany with her knitting, then the creak of the oven door as she opened it. A picture formed in his mind of Naomi standing in another kitchen. Their kitchen.

He was jumping too far ahead. Things were so fragile between them. So tentative.

And yet, he knew their emotions were slowly veering toward a place that gave him hope.

He wished he knew what would happen with Brittany.

CHAPTER 9

"So this is one of the colors of glass I want to use for the grass in the windows," Naomi said, carefully laying the two sheets of verdigris glass she had bought today out on the kitchen table. "If you don't like it, I can get a lighter color."

It was early evening yet. Naomi had returned from her trip to Calgary and Shannon, who had been taking care of Brittany while Naomi was gone, had just left. Brittany was sleeping. She had been extra tired today according to Shannon, but her blood pressure was good, as was her blood sugar.

Shannon and Jess had helped Naomi unload the boxes of glass. Now Naomi was going through them, her heart quickening at the sight of all the colors, her hands almost trembling in their eagerness to start cutting and planning.

She glanced over at Jess, but he wasn't looking at the glass. He was looking at her.

Warmth seeped into her cheeks. Since that evening, when he had brushed her cheek with a kiss she hadn't stopped, everything had shifted between them.

Even though Naomi was still not sure what to think or what to allow, she found her resistance to him and to a relationship with him slowly breaking down. Questions still lingered, but she pushed them aside. Jess might say he's not father material, but what she had seen of his relationship with Brittany, a girl whom he wasn't responsible for, had shone a ray of hope on the shadows of her doubts.

"Looks good to me," Jess said, coming closer. He lifted another pane of glass from the carefully packed box and held it up to the fading light of the sun. "I like the look of the swirls of white in this glass."

"It's supposed to be the snow. I was initially leaning toward glue chip glass because it looks like frost, but I'm using more opalescent than cathedral glass so it will blend better." Naomi carefully lifted another sheet of blue glass out of the box, a frisson of excitement flickered through her as she held it up to the light. "This water glass is one of my favorites."

Jess stepped close enough to look through the glass that she could feel the warmth of his body close to hers.

The whistle of the kettle and Jess's proximity made her lower the glass and hurry toward the stove. "Do you want some coffee?" she asked, disappointed that she sounded so breathless.

"Sure, I'd love a cup. But I can make it."

She waved off his offer. Her hands trembled as she spooned coffee into the press and then poured water over the grounds. She pulled out two mismatched mugs and when the coffee was ready, filled them.

She spooned sugar into her coffee, then handed him the larger mug as he pulled out a chair for her.

With a murmured thanks she sat down and jarred a sheet of glass lying on the edge of the table. It teetered and as she reached for it, she let loose her grip on her mug. She caught the glass, but in the process dumped hot coffee on Jess's T-shirt.

"Oh, no," she cried as he jumped up with a roar, then in one fluid motion, yanked off the steaming T-shirt.

"I'm so sorry," she said. "Are you okay?"

Jess grimaced at the stain on his shirt. "Got the shirt off before it burned me."

He gave her a quick smile, then he bent over and used his T-shirt to wipe up the coffee that had spilled on the floor.

"Here, I'll get a cloth," she said, carefully pushing the sheet of glass back onto the table before getting up.

"I think I got most of it," he said, giving the floor one more quick wipe. Then he turned to the sink, dropped his T-shirt in it and ran the water.

And Naomi stopped and stared.

Two ridged scars, each about six inches long, slashed across Jess's back. Other smaller ones crisscrossed his back below that. She stifled a gasp at the sight.

"What happened here?" she asked, seemingly unable to keep her hand from reaching up and running her finger along the scars. They were hard and angry-looking, a violation on his smooth, tanned skin.

Jess jerked away from her, dropping the T-shirt in the sink as he spun around. "Nothing. It's nothing."

The muted anger in his voice combined with the cold light in his eyes almost made her shiver.

It also made her curious. Why was he so defensive?

"How did you get them? They look bad," she pressed, keeping her voice quiet, as if she was taming something wild.

"It doesn't matter. It's past. He's gone."

"*He's* gone? Are you talking about your father when you say 'he's gone'?" she asked.

Jess turned back to his sodden T-shirt lying in a heap in the sink, ignoring her question as he ran water over the brown stain spreading over the white fabric.

Naomi felt as if she had come against a wall she had often butted against when they dated, and for some indefinable reason she also felt that if she could scale it, she might see into an unknown part of Jess that would help her understand this complicated man.

Again she lifted her hand, her fingers gently tracing the lines of the scars from end to end again and again like they were Braille and might reveal their secrets on their own. "I don't remember seeing these before," she said.

Jess stopped scrubbing at the stain, his head down, his hands growing still. "I got them after you left," he whispered.

"How?"

Jess eased out a heavy sigh, then reached across his chest with his one hand and caught hers, stopping her hand. "Please don't do that," he asked, his voice low and thick. "I don't want you to have any part of them...of how I got them."

Naomi wasn't letting this go, however. She felt as if she and Jess stood on the verge of something important. A shift in their relationship she needed to test.

Then, suddenly, like tumblers in a combination lock, snippets of conversation, memories and thoughts clicked into place, and behind that Connor asking Jess if he still believed all that garbage his father tossed at him.

Jess replying how his father had told him he was worthless and how he wished he had never been born.

Her heart grew cold as she finally understood.

"Your father did this to you," she said quietly, threading her fingers through his.

Jess kept his eyes on her hand, his lips a thin line, then he gave her a tight nod, yes.

"Why?" she asked, only able to choke out that one word past the thickening in her own throat. How could a father do this to his own child?

Jess pulled his hands away from hers, leaning back on the counter behind him for support. "He did it because I threw a party that got out of control. Too many people came over and the house got trashed."

Naomi frowned. "I don't remember you having a party."

Jess lifted his eyes and sent her a dark, broken, longing gaze. "I threw it after you and Billy left for school."

She folded her arms over her stomach, hurt spearing through her. "Because you were happy I was gone."

He released a harsh laugh, laced with anger. "No. Because I couldn't stand the idea that you had left me to go to Billy. Couldn't stand that I might never see you again. I was so full of anger and...and pain at the idea that you were with anyone but me. I was selfish and immature and I figured a wild party would get my mind off you. Trouble was, twenty minutes into the party I knew I had done something monumentally stupid. Things quickly got out of control. I ended up calling the cops. By the time they came it was too late. The house was a wreck. My parents came home the next day and my dad blew up. He yelled at me like he always did, hit me some, then pushed me through the French doors that one of the kids had kicked in. The glass was broken and I fell against it. That's how I got these scars."

"Jess, I'm so sorry. I never knew."

"I didn't want you to know," he said, the bitterness in his voice easing off. "I didn't want you to feel sorry for me like you're feeling sorry for me now." Jess pushed himself away from the counter and gave Naomi a tight smile. "I don't want to talk about my father anymore," he said. "That's in my past. It's over."

"Is it?" Naomi asked.

He frowned at her as if he didn't understand what she was saying.

"I remember how you used to talk about him. How a hard edge would come into your voice that I never understood. Until now. And I hear that same edge now."

"Now you know why."

"I do." Naomi brushed her hand over his back, as if to

remind herself of what had happened to him. "Yet, I also sense that your father still has a hold over you."

"What do you mean?" he snapped.

Naomi tried not to flinch at the lash of anger in his voice, reminding herself of how hard it must have been for him to tell her what he did. At the same time, however, she sensed she needed to gently push on.

"As long as you hold anger in your heart toward your father, he has control, even though he's dead. I think you need to forgive him."

"You saw what he did. This is only a small part of what he did to me. I could tell you about how he would yell at me, how often he raised his fists to me for no reason other than that he could. How can I forgive all that?"

Naomi wished she hadn't started this, but she had and now she had to finish. "It's hard. I know I had to deal with forgiving my father. Once I forgave him, it was easier to let go of my thoughts of him. My anger. I felt like my forgiving him, truly forgiving him, released me from him. Healed me from the pain he gave me when he left. When he abandoned me and my sisters and my mother." She was quiet a moment knowing that being left behind was probably not the same thing as being abused, but it was still a pain she'd had to deal with. She looked up at him, praying he would understand what she was saying. "Forgiveness frees you. It helps you let go of bitterness and anger. It gives you peace and freedom from the person you forgive."

Jess swallowed, his face still set in hard lines, and all Naomi could do was pray that if not now, someday, he would truly understand what she meant.

She touched his arm again, running her hand up it to rest on his shoulder. "I'll be praying that you'll find that peace."

Jess sighed, then looked down at her. She was thankful to see his lips soften into a smile.

"I feel peace when I'm with you," he said quietly.

Her heart beat heavily in her throat at his declaration and she didn't think about his father anymore either.

She didn't know who moved first but it didn't matter, because suddenly her arms wrapped around him, his around her, and as naturally as breathing their lips met.

His lips were warm, soft, inviting. She moaned softly, clinging to him, shifting her lips, trying to get closer.

Her heart beat in time to his, his hand supported her head, holding her close.

Then, finally they drew apart, but Naomi didn't move. Instead she lay her head on his chest, her one hand slipping down to rest on his warm skin. She spread her fingers, encountering another scar, and she bent her head and brushed her lips over it, as if to make it all better.

Then she felt his hand under her chin and she tipped her face up, holding his gaze. He released a soft sigh, then smiled at her, his face holding an expression of hesitancy.

"So now what? What's happening here?" Jess's questions lay between them like a mute visitor that needed to be dealt with.

Naomi eased out a ragged sigh, her lips still burning from Jess's kiss. She reached up to touch her mouth, as if she might find tangible evidence of what had just happened. "I'm not sure."

"I can't act as if that kiss didn't happen," Jess said, his voice a deep rumble beneath her hand. "And I can't go back to where we were before it did."

"I don't want to go back either." And to her surprise, as she spoke the words she knew them to be true. "But I don't know what's lying ahead of us. And I'm scared to go there. What we had before..." Her voice trailed off. She knew she didn't want to delve into a past that had torn them apart, but it seemed to hover, unwilling to leave.

And part of that past was her pregnancy.

Should she tell him now? They had dealt with so much heaviness tonight, she didn't want to bring this into the mix. Not yet. Not when things were so new.

"We were a lot younger then," Jess said, running his hand up and down her arm, his touch gentle. "I know we have a history, but I'd like to think we can start over. We've both had to deal with a lot. We've both changed."

Naomi nodded, still unsure.

Jess tipped her chin up to look at him. "Why don't we try not to analyze it too much? Why don't we take it one step at a time?"

His suggestion wound itself around her heart and she clung to the wisdom of it. Later. She would tell him later.

When he kissed her again, the tiny voice that nagged at the back of her mind was stilled.

"Did you hear that Allison Krepchuk was back in town?" Hailey asked, looking up from the pictures she had brought along.

Naomi shook her head as she carefully traced out the image she had cut out of cardboard onto a new pane of glass. She was working in the living room, the room with the best light. Jess had dragged an old table there for her to work on and a recliner for Brittany to lie in while Naomi worked.

"I've been out of the loop," Naomi said. "And Allison and I haven't written for years. Why did she come back?"

"Heard something about her mother not doing well and a business she started going belly-up." Hailey shrugged. "So she did what we all do when we don't know where we belong anymore. Come home."

Naomi smiled at that. She and Hailey had done the same thing for different reasons.

"Anyhow, I met her at Mug Shots and told her where you were working. Hope that's okay? She said she might stop by."

"Sure. I guess it's okay." Allison was an old friend. It would be good to connect with her again.

Hailey continued flipping through the pictures she had brought along. She pulled one out and laid it on the table Naomi was using to cut the stained glass. "What do you think of this arrangement for the head table?"

"So you're going with Mia for all your flowers?" Naomi asked, glancing at the picture, trying to imagine the arrangement flanking the tables that she assumed would be set outside on the property of Hidden Creek Inn.

"Gotta support that poor girl as much as we can," Hailey said, taking the picture back from her sister. "Single mother with a newborn girl and two boys trying to run a business..." Hailey shook her head. "I don't know how she does it. Besides, she has the most original ideas."

"I think it's cool that you and your sister are having a double wedding," Brittany said from her corner as Naomi showed her the pictures, as well. Brittany shifted herself, trying to get comfortable. "But who is this Allison chick you were talking about?" she asked as she handed Naomi the picture and picked up her knitting again.

"Old friend of mine," Naomi said. "We grew up together and hung out all through grade school and until grade twelve."

"So what happened?"

Jess happened, Naomi wanted to say. All her extra time was taken up with Jess and her friendship with Allison suffered as a result.

"After we graduated we grew apart," was all Naomi said, picking up her glass cutter and fitting it to her hand. She turned the glass she had drawn the pattern on. Then, with just the right amount of speed and pressure, made her cut, the snick of the diamond wheel over the glass giving her a little thrill.

"You always smile when you do that," Hailey said.

"I always feel happy when I do this."

"I haven't seen you smile like this for a long, long time."
Hailey's tone seemed to hold an underlying question Naomi
wasn't ready to acknowledge.

Last night, after Jess left the house, she had sat in the kitchen
for a while, trying to wrap her head around this new situation
and the shift in her emotions.

This morning, when Jess came by with the table, he had been
very matter-of-fact with her. Naomi suspected it had much to
do with being around Brittany.

She had tried not to feel disappointed, reminding herself
that she hadn't completely eradicated her own misgivings about
their being together either.

Then, just as Jess was leaving the house, he stroked her face
with his fingertips, let his hand slide over her shoulder, gave her
hand a squeeze and added a smile that sent her own heart
fluttering.

"I'm glad to be working with glass again," Naomi said, carefully lifting the scored glass and gently bending it at the beginning of the score. She smiled again as the glass made a satisfying
crack, neatly following the score line.

"That's pretty cool," Brittany said. "I thought for sure you
would bust that sucker right in two."

"The score line gives the glass a path to follow." She held the
glass up to check the edge. Perfect ninety-degree angle to the
top. Hadn't lost her touch.

She smoothed the sharp edges with a quick buff of a sanding
cloth, then laid it in place by the other pieces, like adding a piece
to a puzzle.

Hailey got up to get a closer look. "Can't believe you got the
pattern for the first window all planned out already," she said,
bending over the pieces Naomi had already cut and placed.

"I stayed up last night to draw it out and trace it on the
glass." She could feel weariness pulling at her now, but last night
after the kiss she shared with Jess her mind had spun and

tossed. She had read her Bible, prayed, read some more and then, when sleep still eluded her, she pulled out the paper and cardboard she needed and enlarged the window pattern she had drawn up when she had committed to making the windows.

"I know you're glad to be working with glass again, but I get the feeling something else is going on." Hailey looked up at her sister, a gentle frown creasing her forehead, a question in her eyes.

Naomi ducked her head to hide the telltale flush heating her cheeks. Hailey seemed to have a sixth sense when it came to Naomi and her love life, but Naomi wasn't divulging anything willingly.

Hailey glanced over at Brittany who was bent over her knitting, tongue pressed between her lips in concentration.

"Is it Jess?" she whispered.

Naomi pressed too hard on the cutter and the small piece of glass she was working on snapped in three jagged pieces.

"Wow, what happened?" Brittany asked.

"Got distracted," Naomi muttered.

"I hear a car," Brittany said. "I think someone's here."

"I need to clean up this glass." Naomi ignored the knowing look she got from Hailey as she swept the glass onto a dustpan and brought it to the kitchen.

She took an extra moment to catch herself, then as she tossed the glass shards into the garbage, she saw Jess come from his house, striding across the yard. Her heart lifted and she reached up and finger-combed her hair, then caught herself.

Jess kept walking and she heard him call out. Probably to the person who had just arrived.

She stepped out of the door in time to hear a female voice call out. "Hello, son."

Son? Naomi stepped farther out the door and walked around the house in time to see an older woman holding out her arms to Jess.

His mother. Sheila.

She saw Jess give her an awkward hug, the kind you give an aunt you barely know but are expected to greet with more than a handshake.

His mother patted him on the back, then pulled back herself, looking around. Then she caught Naomi's gaze.

"Well, well, Jess did say you were working for him again." Sheila smiled at Naomi as she tottered on impossibly high heels toward her down the broken sidewalk flanking the house. Sheila's short blue jacket, white silk blouse and narrow skirt looked more suited to a high tea than a visit to her son and step-daughter. If that's what this was.

As Sheila came near, Naomi caught an overpowering scent of the woman's perfume and for a moment she was transported back in time to when she used to come and help Jess.

Sheila was then, as now, always dressed like she was ready for her close-up and smelled like a hothouse full of flowers. Naomi always felt gauche and untidy around her. And very, very uncomfortable.

"Hello, Mrs. Schroder," Naomi said.

"Mrs. Anderson," Sheila corrected her. Then she sighed, laying one hand on her chest, shaking her head, not one hair of her perfectly coiffed hairstyle coming loose. "I miss him."

"I apologize," Naomi said, feeling foolish at her mistake. "And I was sorry to hear about your husband's death."

Sheila covered her face with her fingertips and over her shoulder Naomi caught Jess's guarded look. It was as if he wasn't sure what to do about his mother's grief.

Then their eyes met, his features softened and his gentle smile quickened her heart.

Naomi wasn't comfortable with the distance he was keeping between him and his mother. She made a motion with her head toward his mother and gave him a slight frown.

Thankfully he got the unspoken message and came up

beside Sheila and slipped his arm around her shoulder in an awkward motion. "Hey, Mom," he said quietly, giving her a little squeeze. "It'll...you know, it'll be okay."

Sheila lowered her hands and looked up at Jess, surprise altering her features. "Thanks, Jess." She reached up and patted his hand, her surprise shifting into a smile.

Jess gave her another light squeeze, looking a little more at ease this time, but then he came to stand beside Naomi. He slipped his arm around her as well, but this movement seemed more natural and Jess seemed more relaxed than he had looked standing beside his mother.

Naomi caught Sheila's glance, but then an oblique look flitted over her face, as if she wasn't surprised at this turn of events.

"Did you want to see Brittany?" Jess was asking, his fingers tightening on Naomi's shoulder.

Sheila nodded but made no move toward the door. "Do you know when she'll be having her baby?"

"I have to take her to the doctor Monday," Naomi said, trying to sound casual even though she was excessively aware of Jess standing beside her, of his arm over her shoulder. This was the first time he had shown affection to her in front of anyone else.

It felt good and more than that, it felt right.

"He wants to see how things are progressing." She gestured toward the door. "Why don't we all go inside?"

"Of course." But before she did, Sheila glanced over at Jess's house where two men stood on scaffolding slapping stucco on the exterior with quick, practiced movements. "You've come a long way on your house, Jess." Then Sheila sent Naomi an arch look. "I'm guessing you have more incentive to finish it now that Naomi is back."

Naomi couldn't help the flush warming her cheeks, not sure of how to respond to that comment. Things felt so new between her and Jess, she wasn't precisely sure of how to feel and, for once in her life, she was willing to take small steps. See what would happen.

"Why don't we go inside," Jess said, taking Naomi's elbow and gently steering Naomi toward the kitchen door, as if hoping his mother would follow.

"He doesn't like me to say it, but he was always crazy for you," Sheila said to Naomi. "I don't think any of the girls he dated after you left could make him forget you."

Sheila's words settled into Naomi's heart. Naomi didn't want to examine them now, but she knew she would pull them out later when she was alone.

"That'll do, Mother," Jess said, his voice a bit more firm now, but Naomi caught a reassuring tint of pink on his ears.

So Jess could get embarrassed, too.

Brittany was frowning at her knitting when they all trooped into the living room, Hailey bent over beside her, shaking her head, as well.

"Naomi, can you help me with this?" Brittany was saying, turning to look at Naomi. "Hailey says she doesn't know—"

The young girl's voice broke off as her eyes flitted from Naomi to Sheila, her expression one of dismay. Brittany lowered the tiny sleeve she was knitting, swallowed and then said, "What are you doing here, Sheila?"

"I think it's time I go," Hailey murmured, grabbing her purse and patting her sister on the arm as she walked past the small gathering. "I'll talk to you later."

Sheila bustled to Brittany's side, bent over and gave her a quick air kiss, then straightened uneasily when Brittany pulled away.

"Hello, sweetheart. How are you doing?" Sheila said with what sounded like forced cheeriness.

"I'm pregnant," Brittany mumbled, rubbing her index finger over the tip of her knitting needle.

Silence followed this remark.

"My goodness, I didn't know you could knit," Sheila said in that same falsely hearty voice. "What are you making?"

"A sweater. For the baby. Naomi is teaching me." Brittany sent Naomi a pleading look, but Naomi stayed back. Sheila had at least made an effort to finally come. Naomi had to let them figure things out.

"Do you know what the baby is yet? Has Scott gotten hold of you? He's been calling me, you know. I think he misses you." The breathless words tumbled out in a rush as Sheila rested her manicured fingers on Brittany's shoulder.

"I talked to him a couple of days ago and he sent me money. Well, he gave it to Naomi." Brittany ran the wool from the little sweater she was making through her fingers over and over. "But I don't want his money. I want him."

"What will you do when the baby comes?" Sheila asked. "Have you made any plans?"

Naomi tried not to gasp at Sheila's question. She thought Sheila had come back to step up to her responsibility, but the woman's question made it sound otherwise. In her peripheral vision Naomi saw Jess shove his hands in the back pockets of his blue jeans, seeming to make the same assumption Naomi had.

Brittany ducked her head. Naomi wanted to rush over to her side, pull her into her arms and assure her that all would be well.

"Jess said I could stay here." Brittany's voice rose in a question at the end of her statement as if not sure Jess meant what Naomi had heard him promise to her.

Jess nodded once, then looked at Naomi as if seeking her support.

She moved closer and slipped her hand into the crook his arm and gave it a gentle squeeze. She wasn't sure what her role was with Brittany because right now she wasn't sure what was happening between her and Jess. But she knew he needed some show of support.

Sheila shot Jess a surprised look, then settled onto the couch beside the chair Brittany sat in. "Well, that's nice," Sheila was saying, folding her hands one over the other. "That's very kind and generous of him."

And that, it seemed, was that.

Naomi checked her own misgivings, trying not to think too far ahead. Jess had made this offer to a girl who was no relative of his and, by doing so, had shown a deeper love than she had seen in a long time.

She leaned against Jess and looked up at him, suddenly proud of this man and who he was. She didn't know what was in store for them, but for now she would help Jess do what she could. And if that involved helping Jess take care of Brittany...

The implications of that situation caught her short and she wavered a moment.

Was she ready to make that kind of commitment to Brittany and, more important, to Jess?

CHAPTER 10

"Go in peace and may the grace of God our Savior be and abide with you always."

Jess murmured an "Amen" in response to the pastor's parting blessing and as the chords of the last song rang out he clung to the peace that had suffused him throughout the worship service.

In twenty minutes he would be seeing his mother again.

When she showed up on Friday his first reaction was surprise and then, when she said she wanted to stay a couple of days he wasn't sure what to think. While he hadn't wanted to give up on her, he hadn't held out any hope that she would want to be involved with Brittany.

His resentment and anger with his father was also, to a lesser extent, tied up with his mother, as well. While she had never been anything but kind to him, she had also expended so much energy trying to keep his father happy, it was as if she didn't have much time for Jess.

But being around his mother brought back memories of his father. Memories he had spent years trying to erase.

Words from the pastor followed on the heels of those

memories. He had been preaching on the theme of forgiveness and today he spoke of the repercussions of holding on to anger and having an unforgiving heart.

It resonated so well with what Naomi had said, it was almost as if God was trying to tell him something.

How could he forgive his father for what he had done? And would it make a difference?

His father was dead. But his presence still lingered, as did the bitterness his father's abuse had created. Could forgiving his father free Jess from the legacy his father had given him? From thinking he couldn't be a father himself?

A couple of young boys slid past him as he stepped into the aisle, distracting him from his tangled thoughts. Sophie Brouwer smiled a greeting to him.

He pushed his thoughts aside. He didn't like delving into the darkness of his past. He preferred to think of Naomi and the radiance her presence shed on his life.

He felt a light hand on his shoulder and he turned to see Hailey standing behind him. "Hey, Jess. Good to see you here."

"Good to be here," he said, returning her quick smile.

"I heard you sold that cat-skiing operation you used to have," Hailey said as she moved up beside him. They followed the crowd as they slowly made their way out to the foyer, the other conversations around them weaving in and out creating a low-level buzz.

Jess nodded. "Sold it at the end of winter. Working on the ski hill takes up enough of my time."

"You still go mountain biking?"

"Not as much as I'd like."

"What about that souped-up car you used to drive like a wild man around town? Haven't seen that around for a while. You retire it?"

Jess frowned, feeling as if Hailey was interrogating him. "Why do you need to know all this?"

They had come to the foyer, where the crowd had thinned out, and she kept walking so he followed her.

Then she stopped and turned to him. "Yesterday, I saw Naomi happier than I've seen her in years. Even when she was dating Billy."

Why did that send a warm glow through him? But he sensed this was simply an introduction to what she really wanted to talk about. So he folded his arms and waited.

Hailey tilted her head to one side as if studying him. "I know you like to take risks. I know you like to work hard but you also like to play hard. You always did."

Hailey waited a moment, as if expecting a reaction, but Jess pressed back an automatic protest. He wanted to see where Hailey was going.

"What I'm trying to say is Naomi is feeling fragile right now," Hailey continued. "She was completely consumed with Billy and his dying and now she's back here trying to figure out who she is. I know you guys used to date and I know that when you did, Naomi was..." Hailey lifted her hands in a gesture of surrender, as if not sure what words to use. "She was, well, for lack of a better word, incandescent. She shone. She could hardly believe that a guy as popular as you would have anything to do with her. She was crazy about you in a way I never saw with Billy. Then, I don't know what happened, but all she would tell me is that you had a big fight and it was over between you two."

"That was a long time ago," Jess protested, feeling a need to defend himself. He wasn't the only one involved in that particular situation.

"I know. I know." Hailey patted the air between them in a conciliatory gesture. "I guess I'm just saying that after you two broke up, Naomi was heartbroken and devastated." Hailey shook her head and then smacked herself on the forehead lightly with the palm of her hand. "And she would kill me if she knew I was telling you this."

Jess could only stare at Hailey, her words a jumble that didn't make sense.

Naomi? Heartbroken? Devastated? Naomi was the one who'd left him. Naomi was the one who'd gone running back to Billy when he came back to town.

Something was missing in this story.

"Anyway, here's the deal," Hailey continued, charging forward in her usual take-no-prisoners way. "I'm just telling you that you need to be careful with her. Don't play around with her emotions. I know you've changed and that's good, but I also know that in some ways, you're still the same guy. Billy was a good, solid, Christian man. He was the right person for her and now he's dead. I'm scared that she's in an emotionally needy place right now. I'm just looking out for my sister's heart."

Jess couldn't stop the stab of resentment Hailey's warning created. He certainly didn't need the reminder that Billy was the superior man. Jess knew that better than anyone else.

"I care about your sister," he said finally. "She's always been this wonderful, incredible woman. But for now, we're taking things one step at a time."

He didn't want to add that even though Naomi had someone looking out for her heart, he had no one looking out for his. Naomi had broken it once, and he was cautious, as well.

Hailey simply nodded, seemingly satisfied with what he had said. "Okay. Then I guess we'll wait and see how things play out."

She looked like she was about to say more, but then a little girl came bounding up to her, bright red shoes flashing under the layers of her flounced dress. Dan's daughter, Natasha, Jess realized.

"Hailey, Daddy wants you to come downstairs," she said, catching Hailey by the hand and pulling on her. "Aunty Shannon and Uncle Ben are waiting and so is the minister."

Hailey's eyes grew wide with horror. "Oh, no. I forgot about the meeting with the pastor." She shot off a quick wave. "Thanks for listening," she said, then stopped. "And tell Naomi that we're not getting together at Nana's place today."

Jess blinked, trying to get his bearings. Hailey's words confused him but as he walked out of the church, her comments reverberated through his mind. He tried to push back the resentment they caused, but at the same time, he knew he had no right to be upset. He knew he would never be half the man Billy was.

Naomi and Billy had dated for years and in all that time he knew Billy had never allowed himself to get carried away in his relationship with Naomi as Jess had. Billy was the better man and Naomi had chosen him.

Hardly the actions of a brokenhearted girl.

"Hey, Jess." A woman's voice called out again and he spun around, feeling a flash of irritation. He didn't want to talk to anyone right now, but Allison Krepchuk was walking toward him, waving her hand.

He forced a smile to his face as she came closer.

"Hey, Jess. How are things going with you?" she asked, her smile broad, welcoming.

"Good. Really good."

"I heard you're building a new house. That's exciting."

He nodded, wondering where this small talk was going.

Her smile shifted from friendly to forced. "Anyhow, I heard Naomi was taking care of your sister. Is she still there?"

"Yeah. Until Brittany has the baby, that is."

"Good. Okay. Would it be okay if I come up to visit her? I'm only around for another day and I won't have time tomorrow."

He shrugged. "Yeah. Sure. Come on by."

Allison gave him a broad smile and slipped her purse over her shoulder and waited, as if she wanted to say more. But Jess wasn't in the mood for idle conversation, so he pulled his keys out of his pocket and poked his thumb over his shoulder. "I'm sorry, but I should get going. Want to make sure my sister is okay."

"Of course. I'll see you later, then."

He gave her another polite smile and got into his truck, started it and drove away.

His sister was probably fine, but he wanted to double-check. This morning his mother, in a surprising fit of motherly generosity, had offered to stay with Brittany to give Naomi some time off. Naomi had resisted, but now, as he drove back home, Jess had an idea.

When he stepped into the house, all was quiet. He heard the faint murmur of conversation and followed it to the living room.

Naomi was bent over her table, cutting glass, and his mother was curled up on the couch with a magazine.

"So you never did any more of this stained-glass work once you left Rockyview?" his mother was asking, her bright red fingernails flashing as she paged through a glossy magazine.

"I did some, for my art course." Naomi held the piece of cut glass up to the window, smiling as it diffused the light. "But when I switched, no. I was too busy."

Jess clearly heard the regret in her voice and again was so thankful he had asked her to make the windows for him.

He stepped into the room and his mother looked up. "Well, how was church?" she asked.

"The pastor had a good sermon. Thought-provoking."

Naomi's encouraging smile made him glad he had gone instead of staying home as he had originally planned. "What was it about?" Naomi asked, turning back to her glass work.

Jess pursed his lips, thinking, not sure he was ready to discuss forgiveness and mercy in front of his mother. "Well, God, for starters. Sin."

Naomi sent him a wry look over her shoulder. "I would guess those would be some of the main points."

Jess came to stand behind her, looking over her shoulder. From what he could see, she had almost half of the window done already. The glass was laid out like pieces of a puzzle, but he could already make out the snowdrift, the fir trees heavy with snow and the beginnings of the creek. "Wow, that's looking fantastic," he said, feeling a thrum of excitement at the idea that these windows would be in his house.

"It's coming along," Naomi said, stepping back as if to get a better look. She bumped into Jess and he caught her by the arms but didn't let go.

And she didn't move.

He looked down at her head and when he squeezed her arms, he could hear a quick intake of her breath. He wanted to turn her around, pull her close and kiss her.

But his mother was watching them with avid interest, so he simply ran his hands down her arms, then stepped aside.

"I imagine those windows will look even more beautiful once you can see the light coming through them," Sheila was saying.

"The light is what brings them to life," Naomi agreed, bending her head as her hair swung over her flushed cheeks like a curtain.

Jess swallowed and then dropped onto the couch beside his mother. Was Naomi as affected by his presence as he was by hers?

After you two broke up, Naomi was heartbroken and devastated.

Those words had imprinted in his mind and Jess couldn't let go of them.

He glanced around, then frowned. "Is Brittany sleeping?"

"She said she was tired. I'm concerned," Naomi was saying. "I'm glad we'll be seeing Ben, that is, Dr. Brouwer, tomorrow. Her blood pressure is good and her blood sugars are adequate. But I think we need to do a few more tests. She's technically not due for another three weeks, but I'm wondering if Dr.

Brouwer will consider delivering the baby earlier if this keeps up."

He blew out a shaky breath. A baby. What had he been thinking when he gave Brittany the choice to stay here? He knew nothing about babies. He was the last person who should be taking care of a young girl and a baby.

I can do all this through Him who gives me strength.

The Bible passage floated into his mind and settled, easing away the panicky thoughts. He would simply have to do what needed to be done. That was all.

"Are you okay?" Naomi was asking, laying down her cutter. "You look a little pale."

Terror would do that to a person.

"I'm fine. I just need to get out." What he wanted to do was get in that hot rod of his that Hailey had been asking about and tear down some roads like he used to on those days his dad—

He cut that thought off as he held Naomi's gaze. She looked pale, too, which shouldn't surprise him. She had hardly stepped out of the house since she started staying overnight to watch Brittany. The only break she'd had was when she and Hailey had gone to Calgary to look at bridesmaid dresses and when Naomi bought the glass she was working on.

She needed to get out, too.

"Will Brittany be okay for the next couple hours?" he asked, glancing from his mother to Naomi.

Naomi glanced at her watch, then nodded. "She just laid down and will probably sleep for at least an hour, if not more. Why?"

Jess looked over at his mother. "This morning you offered to watch Brittany. Is that offer still open?"

His mother looked up from her magazine, licked her lips, then slowly nodded. "Yes, it is. As long as nothing serious happens. Why? Did you want to go out with Naomi?"

"Yes, I do," Jess said, pushing himself off the couch. He took the cutter Naomi was still holding out of her hand and laid it on the table. "And I think you need to get out of this house for a while."

He squeezed her hand and he could see a flare of hope light up in her eyes.

Then she glanced down the hallway to where Brittany was and she pressed her knuckled fist against her lips as if thinking.

"Shannon has a cell phone, right?" Jess pressed.

Naomi nodded, frowning as if she didn't understand what he was getting at.

"If something happens, my mother can call Shannon. She's a nurse and she's been here before."

Naomi lowered her hand and Jess could see her wavering.

"I'd like to take you up the ski hill on the lifts up to the top of Monihan. There's a great hike that starts there and takes about an hour to go down and this week is the last week we can do it. Come Friday, we're closing the lifts down for maintenance to get them ready for the winter."

He saw a flash of expectant light in Naomi's eyes, but behind that some hesitancy.

"I think that's an excellent idea," Sheila was saying, putting down her magazine and getting up. "And it will give me a chance...an opportunity to spend some time with Brittany, just the two of us."

Jess shot his mother a puzzled look, surprised she would want to do this.

His mother eased out a sigh. "I know I haven't been the most supportive mother to her..." She let the sentence fade away as if unsure of how to finish it. She laid her fingers lightly against her chin, then glanced at Jess. "I'm sorry. I don't think I know how to be a proper mother."

Jess wasn't sure if this was an admission or a confession.

"None of us do," Naomi put in, her voice quiet but holding a faint note of reprimand in it that surprised Jess. Then she took a quick breath. "I think it's important that you connect with Brittany any way you can. You may not feel like a mother, but in her eyes, you are the only mother figure she knows."

To Jess's surprise, his mother nodded. "I know that." She looked as if she wanted to say more, but then gave them a tight smile. "So I'll stay here and talk to Brittany when she wakes up and try not to panic if something goes wrong, and you two are going out and spending some time together."

"Perfect." He left Shannon's cell phone number and before Naomi could formulate another reason to stay behind, he caught her by the hand and tugged her away from the table. "Go and put on a pair of hiking shoes or running shoes and meet me at the truck in about ten minutes."

"Make it five," she said, a bright smile transforming her face.

And it was all he could do not to bend over and kiss her again. Instead, he touched the tip of her nose, like he used to, and left.

"Get ready," Jess said, looking behind as the chair from the chairlift came up behind them.

"This feels weird," Naomi said, moving farther ahead on the platform. Ahead and above her chairs holding bikers and hikers swung from the wire strung between the huge pylons that marched up the hill. "I've only ever done this with a snowboard strapped to my feet and snow everywhere," she said, looking back to center herself on the chair coming their way.

"Ready?" the liftee, a young boy from New Zealand, asked. He held the chair as Naomi sat back, Jess beside her. The chair swung, Jess lifted his hand and brought down the bar that held them in. Then the chair picked up speed and they headed up the mountain, suspended over the ground, the creak and hum of the lift the only noise in the silence that always followed.

Naomi sighed happily and half turned to see the town of Rockyview tucked in the valley behind her, slowly getting smaller and smaller as she and Jess went higher.

"This is so familiar, and yet feels so odd," she said, turning back to Jess. "These hills are supposed to be all covered in snow and I'm supposed to be wearing snow pants, a jacket, helmet and goggles. Not a sweater, shorts and running shoes." She laughed, kicking her feet, making the chair swing, enjoying, more than she thought she would, this unexpected afternoon of freedom. She inhaled a deep breath and looked around, trying to take it all in, memories piling on top of memories.

"Hailey and I used to come out here whenever we could afford it," she said, a huge grin pushing at her cheeks as she looked down at the ground that lay so far below, then up the mountain they were ascending. "Hailey was always more daring than I was, though."

"I remember that," Jess said, leaning back in the chair, his arm slung across the back of it, making it swing. "Not too many people could keep up with her and her kamikaze runs down the hill."

"I sure couldn't. But I still enjoyed it when we could get out here." She turned her gaze back to Jess, drawing in a huge, relaxing breath. "This is fantastic. I feel guilty for leaving Brittany with your mom, but at the same time it's so wonderful to be out here."

Jess threaded his fingers through her hair, lightly caressing the back of her neck. "I'm glad you could come. I was hoping we'd have some time to get away. Just the two of us." His voice held an intimate tone and Naomi couldn't stop a shiver of anticipation at the thought of her and Jess by themselves.

She tipped her head back and let the wind flow over her, lift her hair and tease it away from her face.

"The air smells different up here," she murmured. "Cleaner, brisker, fresher."

"That's only because you've been cooped up in the house for so long."

"I'm also happy your mother offered to stay with Brittany." Naomi's voice grew serious. "It shows that she's willing to acknowledge something of a relationship with her."

"Never my mother's forte," Jess said.

Naomi wasn't surprised to hear the faint bitterness in Jess's voice. The first time they were dating, his mother was around as often as Jess's father—not much.

"At least she's trying."

Jess nodded, then turned back to Naomi. "How about we don't talk about my mother right now? How about we simply enjoy being together alone?"

"Okay, I can do that," she said. Then Jess wrapped his arm around her shoulder and pulled her close. The silence between them seemed peaceful and comfortable and Naomi was content to simply be with this man.

"I have to tell you, I am impressed with what you're doing on the windows," Jess finally said. "They're going to be amazing."

"Of course they aren't turning out exactly like I had in my mind when I first planned them, but so far I'm reasonably happy with them." Naomi followed Jess's lead, realizing they also needed ordinary time together.

If things were going anywhere with them, that is.

Don't go too far ahead, she reminded herself, settling into the space Jess's arm made for her against his side. *You are here, outside on this beautiful day that was like a blessing.*

Don't look too far ahead.

Those words had been her mantra when she was taking care of Billy. She'd had to repeat them to herself so many times. And now, here she was, back in Jess's arms.

And where was that going?

Don't look too far ahead.

"I'm glad you have a chance to do what you love," Jess said, his fingers tracing the curve of her shoulder. "Do you think you'll do more?"

Naomi shrugged, wondering, as well. "Maybe once I get these windows done people who come to your house will be so impressed I'll get some more commissions."

"Maybe," Jess said with a light chuckle. "Though I don't have as broad a social life as I used to. But you could do a few pieces on spec. Display them at the art show they have every month at the old train station."

Naomi's heart fluttered at the thought of working with glass beyond this project. While she was designing the windows, other ideas had come to her and she had to remind herself to stay focused on her current project.

"I remember you saying exactly the same thing when we were...when we were dating."

"And you didn't do anything about it then, so maybe you'll follow my advice this time."

She gave him a wistful smile. "You seem to be more enthusiastic and supportive about my stained-glass work than I've been."

"You look pretty enthusiastic yourself," Jess teased brushing a quick kiss over her forehead. "When I see you cutting and grinding and holding up those pieces to the light, it's like you're lit up from the inside, you look so happy. When I see what you can do with glass, I think you're wasting your talent by not doing anything with it."

Naomi felt a glow deep within her. A glow she hadn't felt in years. "I don't know if I can make a living doing it and right now I still have bills that need to be paid. And after Brittany has her baby, I'm not sure what I'll be doing."

"Maybe this not knowing what you'll be doing is God's way of giving you a chance for you to follow through on all those dreams you used to talk about?"

His question created a gentle warmth in her soul. "You didn't use to talk about God much," she said quietly. "What made you change?"

Jess shrugged and rocked to make the chair swing. "Life. Reality. You used to talk about God and I'll admit, I didn't believe much in Him. Not with the way my dad treated me. Couldn't imagine God as Father when my own dad was...the way he was. But you said something that made me think. That God compares Himself to many things. You said something about Jesus talking to the people of Jerusalem, how He would have wanted to gather them as a hen gathers her chicks. Made me see God in a different light." He was quiet a moment, his fingers gripping Naomi's shoulder a bit harder. "I still struggle with the whole Father thing, but I think I'm getting somewhere."

"I'm so thankful," Naomi said, leaning back into him. Then the chair made another swing and Jess reached up to lift the bar that held them in.

"Not yet," Naomi said, fear twisting her stomach as Jess removed the barrier between her and the void that yawned below them. "It's too soon."

The top of the hill was still thirty yards away and their chair was swinging even more as they approached.

"You're okay," Jess said, "I won't let anything happen to you."

"But—"

Jess squeezed her shoulder. "Don't you think it's kind of exciting to be sitting here, free, with nothing in front of us?"

Naomi clutched his arm. "Hailey used to do that all the time, too, but I never felt as excited about it as she did. I always had to resist the urge to jump."

She could feel the rumble of his laughter in his chest. "I wouldn't let you do that to yourself. I'd stop you."

"Good to know," Naomi said, slowly shifting herself so she was sitting on the edge of the seat, ready to get off when the chair hit the top of the hill.

"The chair goes slower now than it does in the winter," Jess warned her. "Because you can't slide off on the snow, you have to step off—"

But Jess was too late in his warning and as Naomi got off the chair, she stumbled, feeling disoriented at seeing grass beneath her feet rather than snow. She would have fallen but Jess caught her and lifted her away from the chair, then set her down a couple of feet past the lift.

"You okay?" he asked, brushing her hair back from her face in a proprietary gesture.

She nodded, feeling foolish. "Got kind of mixed up there. Thanks for coming to my rescue."

Jess laughed again. Then he turned to look over the valley. "Well, here we are. Which way do you want to go? Blue Run, Green Run, Double Black Diamond? Or take one of the other trails?"

The wind lifted and tossed her hair as she looked down. Below them lay Rockyview, nestled like a tiny jewel in the valley, its streets and buildings like tiny lines and blocks.

She lifted her eyes and looked across the valley. "Oh, look. The Shadow Woman is coming out."

Jess slipped his arm around her waist. "You could always see her before me," he complained.

"That's because I always knew where to look." She leaned against him, sharing the moment, then looked down the run below them.

Large rocks dotted the grass, which made her shiver. "I can't believe we snowboarded over these," she said. "If I had known they were there I wouldn't have gone down those runs. Half the time I only did because Hailey pushed me to do it."

"You didn't know and you went down those runs anyway and everything was fine," Jess said, giving her another squeeze. "Sometimes it's okay not to know what lays underneath."

Jess's words pulled at Naomi's own buried memories and secrets.

She had gotten used to pushing it aside. She had dealt with it and it didn't need to come up. But since she and Jess started spending personal time together, it began hovering on the periphery of her mind, like a dark creature, feeding on her growing relationship with Jess.

You have to tell him about the pregnancy. He has a right to know.

Later. Later. The pain from that loss could still sear, but it wasn't hers only to share.

Her secret loomed large in her mind and would change much. Things were going so well between them. Better even than the first time they were together. She felt more right with him than she ever felt with Billy. She didn't want anything to ruin that.

For now she just wanted to be with Jess. To nurture their growing relationship. She hadn't been this happy in years.

Not since she dated Jess the first time.

"Okay, let's do this," she said, pulling her hair back and twisting an elastic around it, feeling a need to push herself. To keep the secret at bay for a little longer. "Black Diamond it is."

"All right. Just remember, if things get hairy, I'm right beside you."

She gave him a quick smile, his comment underlined by his hand on her shoulder giving her a sense of being cared for. Something she hadn't felt for years.

Then she turned away and started walking.

The sun was warm on her shoulders and the descent more difficult than she had counted on. Soon she was puffing and sweating, fighting momentary bouts of fear as they came upon an especially tricky traverse.

But as the blood coursed through her veins and her heart began thumping in her chest, she felt more alive than she had in years.

"Let's go this way," Jess said, pointing out a cut in the dark, looming fir trees that edged the run, seemingly unfazed by the workout.

Naomi glanced from the open path below them to the trees. "Isn't there a creek that goes through that patch of timber?" The path he wanted to take was out of bounds and although her risk-taking sister had occasionally ducked under the ropes that marked it off to check out the unbroken snow, Naomi, ever the good girl, had never dared.

"Yeah. But we can easily cross it," Jess said.

She stifled her own misgivings, assured by the confidence in his voice, then turned and followed him. The trees enclosed them, towering above them, creating a cool respite from the warm sun. The path leveled out and it was easier going, but Naomi wasn't fooled. She knew they still had to get to the bottom of the hill and it was a long way below them yet.

As she followed Jess, her eyes on his back, Naomi let the peace of the forest surround her. And she and Jess were alone in this quiet.

They went down and down, following the trail. Now and again Jess would point out a plant, a track made by an elk, a scratch in a tree made by a bear. Naomi tried not to think of animals lurking in the deep darkness of the forest, preferring to take her cue from Jess who sauntered along, whistling a tuneless song, unfazed by the prospect of wildlife around them.

She was surprised, however, that she didn't need to talk to Jess. She was content to simply be with him, spending time in God's breathtaking creation.

Naomi slowly relaxed and drew in a long, slow, breath sending up a prayer of thanks. She felt as if the boundaries of her life had fallen into pleasant places. And within those boundaries, she felt the stirrings of hope. Of love?

She looked at Jess, who right at that moment, turned to her, his smile igniting a smoldering of attraction that had been growing between them.

"Thirsty yet?" he asked, waiting as she came to join him.

She nodded, lifting her ponytail off the back of her neck. Jess took that moment to bend over and drop a quick kiss on her lips.

The kiss may have been given lightly, but the look he gave her was anything but. Then he blinked and took a step back, as if to give them space, then held up a finger. "Listen," he said.

Beneath the sighing of the wind through the trees above she heard the sound of running water.

"We're coming to the creek," he said with a cheeky grin. "We'll get a drink there." She returned his smile, the hope she had been feeling earlier deepening.

The trail took a sudden turn and through a break in the trees Naomi caught a glint of silver in the bright afternoon sun. Then they broke into an opening and Naomi came to a complete stop.

The creek that Jess had been talking about was a raging torrent of water tumbling over rocks the size of her. Branches lay crisscrossed on parts of it. And beyond this surge of water she could see where the path continued.

"People cross this?" she asked, aghast.

Jess gave her a puzzled look. "Yeah, all the time."

She held her hands up and took a step back, shaking her head. "Not me."

"It's not hard. Just follow me."

Jess strode on ahead, full of the same bold confidence that had always epitomized everything Jess did. He paused for only a couple of seconds as if to choose his footholds, then took a quick step and another, moving easily from wet rock to wet rock and then he was on the other side. "See?" he called out over the sound of the water. "It's not hard."

"Beg to differ," she called back. She looked at the water, then watched its path as it rushed and splashed down the hill. If she took one wrong step...

She could already see herself stumbling, then falling headlong, down, down, head crashing against the rocks below.

She tried to stop her runaway thoughts but couldn't seem to stifle the vision of herself in a mangled heap a hundred feet down. She swallowed, then looked across at Jess who was waving her on. "You can do it."

Other pictures flashed through her mind from many years ago. Jess convincing her she could take his mountain bike down a steep hill. Jess calling for her to jump into the pool of water at the bottom of a set of falls.

Jess had always pushed and prodded her to try something new. Something different.

Her mind flashed back to Billy, persuading her to switch her art course to something safe. Solid. Secure.

Like him.

Naomi didn't want to be like Billy.

So she took a deep breath, sent up a frantic prayer and took her first step. She wavered a moment, fear choking her, but then she saw Jess, heard his encouraging words and she took another step, then another, following the path he took. Then she looked down.

Dizziness and fear locked her steps. She was halfway across the creek and she couldn't move. Couldn't go ahead, couldn't go back. She heard Jess over the roar of the water and the roar in her ears telling her to make one more step. Her heart fluttered wildly and she wanted to close her eyes, fear immobilizing her. Why did she listen to Jess?

Why did she always listen to Jess?

He's been the cause of your greatest sorrow.

The old words rose up from her fear, but then she heard Jess calling her again and she looked across the water to him. He was holding out his hand, coming toward her.

She took a calming breath, took another step. But her foot slipped on the wet rock. She felt herself slipping.

She was falling.

Panic gripped her and then a strong, warm hand caught hers, pulled her up and she was standing upright, water splashing around her feet.

"I'll help you," he said. She nodded, then, secured by his strong grip, she stepped on the next rock and then the next, following his quiet commands.

Then, amazingly, she was on solid ground on the other side of the creek.

He wrapped his arms around her, holding her close as her heart rate slowed.

"I'm sorry, I shouldn't have made you do this," he murmured.

Naomi let him hold her a moment, just because she enjoyed the feeling of his strong arms protecting her, but then she pulled away, looking back at the river she had just come over.

And then she laughed in pure joy. She had done it. Thanks to Jess, she had faced something she had been afraid of and overcame it. Her heart had been racing, her mind babbling warnings, but she had done it.

Her heart billowed and expanded and her blood sang through her veins. The air around her seemed charged with light and vitality.

She hadn't felt like this in years. Not since the last time she had taken a risk with Jess.

"Are you okay?" Jess asked, tipping her chin up to look at him.

She turned back to him, her laughter turning into a smile of exhilaration. "Jess Schroder, you could always do that to me," she said, catching his face between her hands. "Make me petrified and then make me do something I would never ever do for anyone else."

She grinned, then pulled his head down to hers, planting a kiss on his mouth. "You rock my world," she said.

Jess laughed uneasily, then shook his head. "Well, I could say the same. When I saw you slip and almost fall, I thought this was it. I was so scared."

"I was scared, too. But then you helped me and I made it across." She drew in a long breath, slowing her still-pounding heart. "I made it across and I'm okay."

"The rest of the way is easygoing," Jess said, stroking her now-damp hair away from her face. "No more scary creeks. I'm so sorry."

"You don't need to be. I haven't had that much excitement in a long time."

Jess released a light laugh. "I don't imagine Billy dragged you across creeks that could have killed you. He was always so responsible."

Naomi caught a puzzling note in Jess's voice and what he said seemed to resonate. He had talked like this before. Comparing himself to Billy.

Things were growing more serious between them and she knew that right now, being involved with Jess didn't scare her anymore. But she also sensed that a few things needed to be dealt with before they moved on.

"Come with me," she said quietly, taking his hand and leading him to an open spot in a small meadow beside the creek.

Then she sat down, patted the ground beside her. With a puzzled look, Jess joined her, resting his elbows on his raised knees but giving himself some distance, as if afraid of what she might have to say.

She drew in a slow breath, sent up a prayer for wisdom, then turned to him and said, "We need to talk."

CHAPTER 11

*N*aomi's words sent a flash of dread through Jess. She sounded so serious. What could she have to say that required that frown and that solemn voice?

In the silence following her announcement, he heard the distant screech of a hawk and looked up to see it soaring above them, as if warning him about what Naomi would say.

Was she now going to tell him that she was changing her mind about being with him? That after risking her life crossing some stupid stream she realized that Jess was not the man for her?

He wasn't ready to go there yet. Not when he was falling for Naomi even harder than he had before.

"So tomorrow you're taking Brittany to the doctor?" he asked, hoping to forestall anything she might have to say.

Naomi gave him a puzzled look but then nodded, thankfully willing to go along with his diversion for now. "I'm worried about her, but everything seems to be going well otherwise. It's just a feeling I have."

"I hope she has a normal delivery," Jess said, tapping his thumbs together.

The following silence seemed heavy, then Naomi spoke up.

"I think it's remarkable that you took her in," she said quietly. "You didn't have to. You could have told your mother to find someone else."

"Couldn't turn her out on the street," he protested.

"As if you would," Naomi said with a hint of irony.

"Probably not. Though I'm not sure how I'm going to handle things once she has the baby." He blew out his breath. "I'm nervous about it. Like I said before, I'd make a lousy parent."

"You know your words say one thing but your actions say another." Naomi rested her hand on his arm. "You're doing what your mother couldn't and, I'm guessing, what your father wouldn't."

Jess shrugged off her comments. "Doesn't matter. When it comes time for that baby to find a place, I wish it didn't have to be mine."

"Even though you feel this way, you're still thinking of letting Brittany come back to your place with that baby."

Jess sighed. "Yeah, but I'm still scared."

"Why?"

Her single word hung between them and Jess eased out a heavy sigh. "We covered this already."

"I think you need to talk more about this."

Jess caught the back of his neck with his hand. He didn't want to go back to a past he'd spent so much time trying to eradicate from his memory.

"Why are you scared?" she urged.

Jess sighed. Here we go again, but this time, to his surprise, he felt a little less leery about giving Naomi a glimpse into his life. He'd spent so much time hiding what his father did and hating him for what had happened that it was starting to define him. Maybe it was time to let everything out into the open. Into the light.

"Those scars on my back you saw weren't the only ones he gave me," Jess said quietly. "All my life I've had to hear how stupid I was. How useless. He'd get mad, slap me around, and that hurt. But the worst were the times he'd yell at me that he wished I was never born. I always wondered why he hated me so much. Why he talked like that. Turns out his dad did the same thing to him. And so did his grandfather to his father. The Schroder men are mean, selfish and nasty with bad tempers." Jess clenched his fists, looking down at them as if wondering if they would betray him, too. "It gets passed down, you know? I've read about that. Children of abusers become abusers themselves. I don't want to put any kid of mine through that. I don't want to make any kid in my life go through the humiliation and pain I did. I don't want to subject any child to what I've had to deal with." He released a short laugh. "You know that for yourself. You saw me in action."

"What are you talking about?"

The puzzlement on her face surprised and confused him. How could she not remember?

"That fight we had. When we both decided we wouldn't let ourselves fall into the trap of letting our relationship just be physical. Then you started talking marriage, which was okay with me, but then you brought up kids."

She lifted her knees and wrapped her hands around them, nodding as if she remembered now. "I remember getting angry with you because I thought you were looking for a reason to push me away."

"Why would I do that?"

Naomi's cheeks turned pink and she looked away, her hair, now loose, flowing over her cheeks, hiding her expression. "Because I thought you saw me as cheap after what happened. I thought you didn't want to have anything to do with me. And I was... I was afraid because—"

143

"You were afraid of me," was all he said with a bitter laugh. "The look on your face when I got angry will stay forever branded into my memory. I wanted to stop yelling at you but I couldn't. I couldn't because I was scared." His words came out on a rush of guilt he had carried with him ever since she had taken those scrambling steps away from him. He rested his head in the palms of his hands as if the story weighed so heavily on his mind, he needed help to hold it up. "When I saw you, with your hands up in the air as if trying to protect yourself from me, I realized at that moment I had turned into my father. And I realized I was nothing like Billy. So I pushed you away the only way I could. With my anger. When I found out that you were back with Billy, I knew I had done the right thing. You belonged with him. He was the person I could never be."

A soft wind moaned through the trees above and the water beside them kept flowing and rushing down the hill, relentless, ever-moving.

"Billy was a good man and he was good to me." Naomi pulled her knees close to her chest again, as if protecting herself. "When I went back to Billy I thought I was doing the right thing. After all, Billy and I had dated all through junior high and high school before I met you." She leaned forward, resting her chin on her knees. "When I was with him, I thought I knew what love was. Then I met you." She paused, then gave him a quick sidelong glance. "I always thought you were good-looking, but then, so did most of the girls in Rockyview High. I never, ever thought you would be interested in someone like me."

"What? How could you say that?"

She tilted her head, giving him an "are you kidding" look. "I grew up in the shadow of Hailey, my more vivacious, sister, and Shannon, who was the most organized and capable person you'd ever meet. My fellow classmates were girls ten times more beautiful and confident than me. I was just Naomi. So when Billy wanted me to date him, I felt wanted. I felt needed. And we were happy together. Billy was a good Christian man who was good to me."

Jess kept his comments to himself. He didn't want to find out this much about Billy, but he sensed Naomi had to get this out.

He thought back to what Hailey had told him this morning in church—warning him about Naomi's loss. As if he needed to be reminded.

"When we, you and I, were together, I felt like I was caught in a whirlwind of emotions and feelings," Naomi continued. "I felt like I was trying to keep up to you."

"I'm so sorry," he said. "I wish I could tell you how sorry I was that I pushed you that night. That I... That we..." He sighed, shoving his hand through his hair.

She looked at him again, a frown furrowing her brow, and was that a glint of tears in her eyes?

Her lips trembled a moment and then she put her hand on Jess's arm and to his shock and amazement, she leaned close and laid a gentle, heart-searing kiss on his lips.

"What happened, happened to both of us," she whispered, pulling back enough to look into his eyes. She blinked and a tear slid down her cheek. "It was both of us who were involved, both of us who got carried away." She kissed him again and then moved closer, leaning against him.

"I don't want to make the same mistake again," he said.

"We won't," she said quietly.

He wrapped his arms around her, as if afraid she would disappear on him as she had so often in the dreams that tormented him after she left with Billy.

"I should have—"

"*We* should have," she corrected. "Please, let's not talk about that anymore." She eased out a sigh. "I want you to know that when I went back to Billy, I felt lost. Lonely and afraid." She stopped there, pressing her fingertips to her lips, as if holding something back. "Anyway, we dated and did all the things that we should. We had devotions together and we studied together and then, when he proposed to me I thought this was a natural progression. He wanted to wait until we paid our debts off and I was fine with that. We were engaged for over four years and I was okay with it." She nestled closer to him. "But the whole time I was with him, I felt as if something vital was missing. I told myself the feelings I experienced around you were the feelings of an adolescent girl caught up in the magic that was you. But I never forgot you. I never forgot how alive I felt around you. And I knew what I felt for Billy wasn't anything close..." She drew in a long, slow breath. "I finally decided that I had to break off the engagement. Billy hadn't been feeling well, so I thought I would wait until he felt better. Then, just when I figured I had found the right time, he came back from a doctor's appointment to tell me he was diagnosed with malignant bone cancer. Inoperable. He probably had only a year to live. I knew I couldn't break up with him then. So I stayed with him and I took care of him. I quit my job the last six months so I could be with him all the time." Her hands tightened on Jess's arm. "But I never forgot about you. Never."

Jess let the words settle into the empty, dry spots of his soul as he gently turned her face toward him. His eyes traveled her features, a face that had haunted him for years. She remembered him. She thought about him.

"So you didn't walk away as freely as I thought?" he asked.

She shook her head. "I felt like I had no choice. Billy came back and he was asking me to come back and I was... I was—"

Jess was tired of talking about Billy and the past. He stopped her words with a kiss. Then another. He cupped her face and rained kisses over her cheeks, her eyes, her chin, then pressed one more to her lips.

She eased out a sigh and nestled into his shoulder.

"I'm sorry, Jess. I'm so sorry."

He shushed her and wrapped his arms around her. "No more apologies. No more looking back. We're together now. Right here, right now. Let's not get bogged down anymore. I want to think about the future."

"I'd like that," Naomi said.

"You know that I'm falling for you."

"I kind of guessed that," she said, her voice holding a note of humor. "You know I'm feeling the same."

Her words wrapped themselves around his lonely heart. "I know we've been here before, but I also know that it feels different this time. Richer. Deeper." He stopped there, afraid he might run too far ahead of her.

"I care about you more than I've ever cared about anybody," Naomi said quietly, her hand running up and down his arm. "I want to see where this will take us. I want to be together."

He couldn't say anything to that so he simply brushed a gentle kiss over her temple, then held her close.

They sat this way a moment longer, then a cloud drifted across the sun and the air cooled.

"We should probably get going," Jess murmured, the first one to draw back. He got to his feet and reached out to pull Naomi up, but she stayed where she was, not looking at him, her hand fiddling with the gold nugget hanging around her neck.

"Is everything okay?" he asked, concern niggling at him.

She pulled her hands over her mouth, then looked up at him, her face holding a mixture of fear and sadness that made his heart stutter. "Before we go, there's something else I need to tell you."

Naomi's voice was a tiny, quiet sound and Jess felt like he would have to brace himself. What else could she possibly have to say?

Then his phone rang, the silly song he had chosen almost

mocking the moment. He wanted to ignore it, but with his mother watching Brittany, he didn't dare.

So in spite of the feeling that he had dodged something important, he glanced at the phone. It was his mother.

"Hello," he said, his eyes on Naomi, who was now looking down, her hand on her heart.

"It's Brittany," his mother said, her voice breathless with fear. "...coming..." The call cut out and Jess wanted to shake the phone.

"Is the baby coming? Is that what you're trying to say?"

"...called an ambulance..." was all Jess heard. Then the phone went dead. He glanced at the handset only to be informed that the call was dropped.

He glanced at Naomi. "It's Brittany. My mom called the ambulance."

Naomi's heart was pounding faster than the rhythm of her feet as she and Jess jogged down the mountain, tree branches slapping her face. Jess was constantly checking his cell phone, hoping for reception, but Naomi was sure they wouldn't get anything until they got to the bottom of the hill. She prayed as she ran.

Please, Lord, let everything be okay. Please let Brittany and the baby be okay.

She couldn't let her mind go any further than that.

Every curve in the trail, every rise, made her want to cry out in frustration. It took forever to get to the bottom.

She ducked to avoid a branch, then jumped across a spring of water. Slowly, the trees grew more spaced out, the incline decreased and finally, they broke out into the open. To their far right she could make out the buildings of the ski lodge situated at the bottom of the hill.

Jess pulled out his cell phone as Naomi caught up to him, but then he shoved it back in his pocket. "It's dead," he said with disgust. He turned and started running across the grass toward the chalet.

Naomi followed, barely able to keep up with his long legs. They ran past the pylons from the first ski lift, then past the T-bar for the bunny hill. Jess was almost a hundred feet ahead of her, his feet clattering down the metal stairway to the chalet. He went around the back, pulling his keys out of his pocket. He unlocked a door marked Private and went inside.

Naomi stopped a moment at the top of the stairs, a stitch in her side as she bent over, catching her breath. Then she followed Jess.

He was talking on the phone when she stepped inside the office, the sound of the door closing echoing in the empty room.

A large desk filled one corner of the room and beyond that was another door. A nameplate beside the door still held Jess's father's name.

"So what did the paramedics say?" Jess was asking. He looked over at her and gave her a wan smile, his chest heaving.

"Okay, we'll be there in a bit," he said, biting out the words.

He dropped the phone into the cradle and leaned back against the old oak desk, pushing his damp hair away from his face. "False alarm," he said breathlessly. "Brittany just had a minor panic attack. And, I guess, so did my mom." He took a few more deep breaths, his hands resting on the edge of the desk. "Are you okay?"

"I'm fine now," she said, her heart pounding with a mixture of fear and exertion. "Out of breath, but thankful that Brittany is okay."

"Me, too." He pushed himself away from the desk, his face set in hard lines. "Let's get back to the house."

Naomi wondered why he was so angry and barely managed

to keep up with him as he strode across the grounds of the ski hill toward the parking lot where his truck was.

A few minutes later they headed down the road leading toward the highway to town. Jess was staring straight ahead, saying nothing, his eyes narrowed, his fingers drumming the steering wheel.

"Did your mom say what triggered the attack?"

"I guess Scott called."

"Did she say what it was about?"

Jess gave a tight shake of his head. "No. Only that after he called, Brittany called my mom. Said her heart was racing and she couldn't breathe. My mom panicked and called the ambulance. I'm guessing that little weasel didn't have good news for Brittany."

Naomi felt a jolt of disappointment both for Brittany and, yes, for the young man she had met only the one time. "When he approached me at church that one Sunday, I was so hoping it was the first step toward reconciliation with Brittany."

Jess spun the steering wheel as he turned onto the road heading up to his house. "I was, too. Guy should step up. Take responsibility for his actions."

Naomi's heart stuttered in her chest as she realized that Scott was the source of his anger.

Tell him now.

But as she glanced over at the anger etched on his face, she knew she would have to wait a bit longer.

As Jess made the final turn, Naomi saw an unfamiliar car parked in front of the old house. The ambulance was already gone, but who was visiting? A friend of Sheila's?

She groaned. This was not a good time to entertain company. Couldn't Sheila see that?

Jess parked the truck by his house, turned it off and blew out his breath. "Glad you were with me," was all he said, giving her a tight smile. "Now let's go see what's up with Brittany." Then he jumped out of the truck and strode toward the house.

Naomi got out, wondering when she would find the time to talk to him if Sheila or Brittany was having visitors.

She stepped into the house via the kitchen door. Jess was talking to Sheila and sitting at the table with her, cradling a cup of coffee was Allison Krepchuk. An old friend of Naomi's.

Allison looked up from her coffee, then got up, her arms out. "Hey, Naomi. How are you?"

"It's been ages." Naomi hugged her friend, then drew back to look at her. "I'm good. How about you?"

She knew Allison was back in town through Hailey. She simply hadn't the time or energy to connect with her. And now she was here at the most inappropriate time.

But she went automatically through the steps of greeting and asking, being polite despite internally seething with frustration. It had taken her so long to work up the courage to talk to Jess and it seemed that events were conspiring against her. And now she had to make small talk with Allison. Though she was glad to see her friend the timing sucked.

Allison shrugged and gave her a quick grin. "I'm okay. I'm glad to be home. And you? Sheila was telling me you're taking care of Brittany."

"Where is Brittany?" Jess was asking his mother.

"She's sleeping," Sheila said, giving Naomi a quick smile.

Naomi was distracted by the questions Jess was asking his mother and said nothing more to Allison.

"So what did Scott have to say to her?"

Sheila's smile was even more confusing. "It was good news. He said he wants to be involved with the baby. He said that he's working on getting a place for Brittany and the baby, but that it would take a month." Sheila pressed her hand to her heart. "Brittany was so overwhelmed, her heart was pounding. She could hardly talk. I got scared, so I called the ambulance and then I called you. Don't know what came over that girl."

Or you, Naomi wanted to say. Obviously Brittany was okay. It was Sheila who had overreacted.

"So you called the ambulance?" Jess asked, his voice heavy with incredulity.

"Well, I didn't know what to think. I know she's not well and that she's fragile. I guess I—"

"Panicked," Jess finished for her, giving Naomi a weary glance. Then, as if noticing her for the first time, he looked over at Allison. He gave her a polite smile, said hello, then walked down the hall to Brittany's room.

Allison caught Naomi by the hand and pulled her down onto a chair across from her. "Sit down. Tell me more about your life. What's been going on since you and Billy left Rockyview?"

"Would you like some coffee, Allison? Naomi?" Sheila was asking.

Naomi nodded as she watched Jess disappear into Brittany's room. She was tired and her whirling thoughts finally began to settle and find their place in her aching head. She wanted to be alone with him, but right now Allison was claiming her attention.

"So I heard about Billy," Allison was saying. "I'm so sorry. That must have been hard." She claimed Naomi's hand, squeezing it lightly.

"It was," Naomi admitted. "But I am thankful God has given me the strength to deal with it. And every day is a new day." Sheila set a cup of coffee in front of her and patted her on the shoulder, as if commiserating with her as well.

"And how is your nana?" Allison asked. "I heard she had a heart attack last fall?"

"She was one of the reasons I came back."

Allison glanced back over her shoulder to Brittany's room

where Jess now was, lips shaping a tiny smirk. "I'm guessing there was another reason you came back?"

Naomi chose to ignore the innuendo in Allison's voice. Allison knew all about Naomi's relationship with Jess. It was one of the reasons their friendship faded. Allison had never approved of Jess and had made her views known loud and clear.

"Hailey and Shannon are getting married," Naomi said. "And I wanted to be around for that, as well."

"Are you thinking of sticking around Rockyview awhile after the weddings?" Allison continued.

Naomi couldn't stop a faint flush that tinged her cheeks, thinking of the kisses she and Jess had shared up on the mountain. "I'm fairly sure I am."

"And Jess is building a new house," Allison was saying, as if there was a connection between the two statements. Which there was, but Allison didn't need to know that right now.

"Naomi is making stained-glass windows for it," Sheila put in.

Allison turned back to Naomi, her features holding genuine pleasure. "That's fantastic. I was always surprised you didn't do more with that. You were so good." Allison turned to Sheila. "She's done some great stuff with her stained-glass work. My mom got her to do some lamps. She still has them. Has been offered a lot of money for them, but she won't sell them."

"The windows are just a project for now," Naomi said.

Allison poked her, a knowing smirk on her face, as she leaned forward. "If I'm not mistaken, it looks like you and Jess are back together again?"

"They went for a hike this afternoon," Sheila put in helpfully. "A date."

Naomi wanted to roll her eyes, but Allison was looking at her, surprise all over her face. "Really?" Then she sat back, taking another sip of her coffee. "You know, despite what I always said about him I think it's a good thing. I realize now that you and Jess belong together. I never saw you so happy with anyone as when you were with Jess. I think it's great that in spite of everything that happened with you and him, you guys are back together."

Naomi's heart stammered in her chest. "What do you mean 'in spite of everything that happened'?" Confusion mingled with fear.

What exactly was Allison talking about?

The door to Brittany's room opened and shut and Jess came walking down the hallway.

But Allison didn't seem to hear Jess coming and leaned forward, her voice growing more quiet. "You know. What happened after you and Jess, you know, were together. I don't know what I would have done in your case. That must have been so hard." She put her hand on Naomi's arm, the concern in her gaze and the sympathy in her voice sending a chill through Naomi's heart.

Was she talking about the pregnancy? If so, how in the world did she know? Naomi had told no one but Billy. Not even her sisters knew then.

"How did you know? How did you find out?" The questions burst out in a panicked rush.

"Billy told me that he—" Allison began.

"Billy told you?" Naomi interrupted, the chill turning to ice. "He shouldn't have. What happened was personal. Private." Even as she protested, her mind scrabbled back. Had she told Billy? She had been so ashamed. She was fairly sure she had said nothing to him.

"But...everyone knew," Allison said, her expression one of genuine confusion. "I mean, the whole town knew that when Billy came back and found out you were dating Jess, he was determined to get you back."

Dread clutched her heart as Naomi realized what Allison was talking about. She pressed her chilly fingers to her lips, stilling anything more she might say, knowing she had already said too much.

Please, Lord, help me get through this.

Then, as she looked at Jess's expression, she knew the time had come. She couldn't put this off any longer.

CHAPTER 12

*J*ess stared at Naomi who now sat back in her chair, her eyes closed, her fingers pressed to her lips.

What did she mean when she said it was personal and private? *What* was?

The questions circled his brain and even though he tried to tamp them down, he knew he would be asking them of Naomi when the time came.

"How is Brittany?" Sheila was asking him, seemingly unaware of the emotions swirling around the other occupants of the room.

"She's okay. She wasn't sleeping," Jess said, the mental switch in gears almost making his mind crunch. "She was telling me about Scott when he called again. Sounds like they're making plans."

"Well, isn't that wonderful," Sheila was saying with what looked to Jess like a relieved smile.

"Yeah. Pretty good." He had felt a moment of relief, as well, but that had only lasted as long as it had taken him to walk from Brittany's room to the kitchen.

When he heard Naomi's scattered comments and saw the

sheer panic on her face. What was she so afraid of? What had Allison said that triggered it?

"It's okay," Allison was saying, patting Naomi on the arm. "You and Billy had dated for ages. I mean, when he came back to town after you and Jess got together, none of us were surprised you went back to him. Though I thought your sisters knew about it. I mean, the whole town knew about it."

"Of course. Yes, they did," Naomi said, breathless, her eyes downcast. "I meant that they didn't know...didn't know why... Anyway, it's all in the past now."

"Yeah, it is. And for the record, I always thought you and Jess made a better couple." Allison glanced over at Jess, giving him a quick smile. "And I'm happy for you that you guys are back together again."

Jess gave her an absent nod, glanced over at Naomi again, who still wasn't looking at him.

Curiosity gnawed at him, but he guessed he wouldn't learn anything more until Allison was gone.

"I'm going over to the house to get a few last-minute things done," he said to his mother.

"Connor phoned, as well," his mother told him. "He said he would be done tomorrow. And some guy left a message about the soffit and fascia, whatever that is."

Jess acknowledged his mother's information with a tight nod. That meant that all the last-minute things would be done earlier than he thought. The house would be officially done tomorrow.

So why didn't he feel happier about that?

He walked out of his old house and headed toward his new house, Naomi's strange behavior nipping at his insecurities. Just relax, he told himself. She's feeling overwhelmed after what happened, or rather didn't happen, with Brittany, that was all.

He was feeling overwhelmed himself. One minute he thought Brittany was having her baby, the next minute the father of the baby was stepping up to his responsibilities. His relief made him feel guilty, but at the same time he was thankful things were coming together for Brittany.

He stepped inside his house, the smell of new carpet and paint still present. He smiled as he looked around the first floor. The hardwood floors of the living and dining room were an expanse of gleaming oak, waiting for tables, couches, lamps and chairs to soften them. The kitchen cabinets shone with a dull glow, the brushed-metal pulls the exact complement to the walnut stain. The bricked-in archway for the stove stood empty, as did the space for the refrigerator. Those appliances were coming tomorrow and then he would have to think about furnishing the rest of the house.

He had put that off for the past few weeks.

In some tucked-away corner of his mind he had nurtured a faint hope that Naomi would be having some say in how they furnished it.

But now?

He tamped down the misgivings he had felt when he saw Naomi's reaction to what Allison had said a few moments ago.

Please, Lord, help me to let go of what I can't control and trust in You.

The prayer settled him and as he went up the stairs, his eyes shifted to the space that would soon hold the stained-glass windows Naomi was still working on. He smiled at the thought. Everything will be fine, he told himself.

Just fine.

Naomi walked Allison out to her car, hoping her friend didn't think she had gone completely off the deep end. Partway through the visit Sheila had excused herself, but not before giving Naomi a decidedly puzzled look.

Naomi didn't blame her. The words that Naomi had spilled out when Allison had made her innocent comment would confuse anyone. She had also caught the surprise on Jess's face. She wanted to run to Jess and explain.

But Allison had wanted to see the stained-glass windows, so Naomi showed them to her, trying to keep up her end of the conversation about old friends and how wonderful it was that Naomi was doing what she loved and would Naomi consider doing some more work for Allison's parents?

Naomi wanted to get excited about the idea, but all the while in her head Naomi kept revisiting the conversation they'd had when Jess came down the hall.

Allison hadn't known about the pregnancy, she realized. It was Naomi's own inherent guilt that had made her overreact to what Allison was saying. That and the fact that she needed to tell Jess about the pregnancy had been roiling below the surface of every conversation she'd had with him for the past few days.

She needed to find out more, one part of her mind reasoned, even as she made inane chitchat with Allison. She needed to know his reasons for why he always said he didn't want to be a father.

But even as one part of her mind excused herself, her conscience accused her.

Jess had a right to know much sooner than now. And once Allison was gone, she had to talk to him.

"So can I let my parents know?" Allison was asking.

Naomi yanked her thoughts back to her friend, trying to catch up.

"About the windows I asked you to make for them," Allison prompted, giving Naomi a puzzled smile.

"Yeah. Sure." Naomi gave herself a mental shake. "Let me know when it's convenient to talk to them and...and I can come over."

"I'll do that." Allison gave Naomi a quick hug. "It's so great to see you again and, to tell the truth, I'm so glad you're back with Jess. He and you belonged together way more than you and Billy."

Naomi wanted to ask her more about her comment, curious why she should say that when she and Billy had dated so long, but she simply returned Allison's hug, gave her a quick smile, then bade her goodbye.

She waited until Allison's car rounded the corner, then turned to face Jess's house.

Please, Lord, help me say the right thing, she prayed, her chilly fingers wrapping themselves around each other. *Forgive me for waiting so long. Help me to find the right way to tell him. Open his heart to what I have to say.*

Then she blew out her breath, took another one and strode up the sidewalk to the house. She stepped inside and heard Jess's tuneless whistle coming from upstairs. He always said he couldn't hold a tune, but he loved music.

She called his name and waited but didn't hear a reply. Her heart was knocking so hard, she was surprised that didn't draw his attention.

She followed the sound of his whistling, on one level admiring the craftsmanship of the house, allowing herself a tiny glimpse of hope. Would this be their home?

She walked up the stairs, her hands clammy on the wooden rail and when she came to the top, he stepped out of a room. He gave her a quick smile and walked over to her and gave her a hug.

"Good news about Brittany, eh?" he said, running his hands up and down her arms.

She nodded.

"I'm so glad Scott is doing the right thing. I hope he and Brittany can make it work. It's a tough start with a baby right away. I know I would have a hard time with that." He stopped and released a shaky laugh. "Sorry, I'm yapping away here."

"Would you have?" she asked, latching on to his previous comment. "Would you have had a hard time if you had to deal with a baby right away?"

Jess nodded. "Yeah, I would. I've told you enough times how I felt about kids. About being a father."

"Yet you offered to take Brittany in. And you said she would have a home if she and the baby needed it."

"Of course. But, really, it wouldn't have been my kid, so I think that's different." He frowned, a concerned light in his eyes. "Why are we talking about this?"

Naomi felt her resolve falter, then winged up another prayer and wished they were sitting down. Not standing in a hallway, their words echoing in the empty house.

"I have something I need to tell you and I'm hoping, no, I'm praying you'll understand."

"Does it have to do with what you were saying to Allison?"

"Yes, it does."

Jess's only reply was to cross his arms.

"I suppose you remember the fight you and I had?" she continued. "Before I went back to Billy?"

"Yeah." He dropped the word like a rock between them. "How could I forget? I can't apologize enough for what happened then—"

"You talked about how you didn't think you could be a father and now I know why." She licked her lips and locked her hands. "I'm sorry I never completely understood what you had to deal with. I never... I never knew how hard it was for you."

Jess said nothing, his feet planted on the carpet, as if bracing himself.

"The reason I had come to you to talk about being a father, about being married was because...when I came to you...well...I was pregnant. Pregnant with your baby."

The words she'd been storing up for weeks, maybe even

years, finally spilled out into a silence so deafening it made her ears ache.

Then she dared look up at Jess and the anguish on his face tunneled into her soul.

"I know I should have told you, but it was so hard," she said. "It was like I kept the secret so long it became a part of me. It became normal and I didn't see you. Didn't expect to see you until I came back here. Then, spending time with you...I fell in love..."

Naomi tamped down the words roiling beneath the surface. The words that would pull her back into a storm of feelings she always experienced around Jess. Words that would pull at the frail grip she had on her fragile self-control. She had to stay in charge.

"So how did you break the news to Billy?" Jess said. "Or did you and him—"

"No. Never. I told you when I first came here that you were the only one I was ever, ever intimate with." She wished she didn't sound so defensive, but Jess had no right to accuse her of what he just did.

"I'm sorry," he said, shoving his hands through his hair, his face twisted into an expression of anguish. "I shouldn't have said that."

Then he looked at her, his eyes blazing with intensity. "So where's the baby? Did you give it up?"

Naomi shook her head, the old pain surging up from where she thought she had buried it. "I miscarried at three months."

Jess was silent a moment, as if acknowledging the sorrow she had dealt with.

Then he looked at her again. "Why didn't you ever say anything? Why didn't you tell me?"

Naomi wished she didn't have to dredge up the memories of the day that sundered her life into Jess and After Jess, but they had to finish this.

"It was hard for me. I always felt as if it was a miracle you were even remotely interested in me. You could have had any girl you wanted, yet you chose me."

Jess's frown told her that he still didn't truly understand how she saw herself.

"I was afraid and young and foolish. I was also pregnant and alone. Then when we had our fight about you not wanting to be a father, I got scared. I didn't think you would accept this baby and I was only eighteen. Then Billy came back and said he had made a mistake, I thought it was my chance. It was so hard for me, Jess."

He stared at her shaking her head.

"Do you think it was easy for me?" he asked, stepping closer as if trying to dominate her by his nearness, his very maleness. "You say I could get any girl I wanted, well, I never wanted anyone but you. You were the best thing that happened to me. You were like a bright and shining light in my lousy existence. You were the first person I was ever with who gave me some ray of hope that I could have an ordinary life. Then I had to watch you run back to Billy and leave with him and leave me behind. And now I find out you were expecting my child?"

"A child you said you didn't want," she protested. "When we talked about parenthood you lost it. You were so vehement. We fought about it and I was terrified that I would end up being alone, abandoned by you. That was why I ran back to Billy. Because I was pregnant and afraid and you said you would never be a father to the child I was carrying. What was I supposed to do?"

Jess's eyes narrowed, his jaw clenched and Naomi could see a hardness grip his features that froze her heart. "I never said I didn't want *that* child. I didn't think I could be a father. I still don't think that, but I would have dealt. I would have stepped up. You should have given me the chance to find out instead of running back to Billy." Then his eyes grew bleak. "Would you have said anything if Allison hadn't pushed you? If you hadn't believed she knew? How long were you going to wait to tell me?"

Naomi felt the ground she had stood so firmly on since she left Jess shift and heave. She had always assumed that Jess didn't want to be a father. He had made it so clear. Knowing why didn't change the fact that he had consistently said the same thing.

Now he was saying he could have dealt?

"I was afraid, too," Naomi said, her voice faltering. "I was afraid to tell you. Afraid to even acknowledge to myself what had happened. I've always been the good girl. The one who keeps everyone happy. The one who never does anything wrong. I didn't even dare tell my sisters. They didn't know and the longer I waited the harder it got."

Jess just stared at her. "So who did know? About our baby?"

"Billy."

He took a wavering step backward. As if that single word was a blow that hit him with the same force his father's fists had.

"Of course," was all he said.

He drew in a deep breath, closed his eyes and when she reached out to him, he sidestepped her.

"I gotta go," was all he said.

Then with each footfall echoing in the yawning emptiness of the house, he walked down the stairs and out of the house.

She was going to have a baby.

She was going to have *his* baby.

She couldn't tell him and then she lost it.

Jess rammed his truck into overdrive, spun around another corner, almost fishtailing on the gravel as he headed down the hill. He didn't know where he was going. Somewhere away from Naomi and the news she had dropped like a bomb into his life.

I got pregnant.

Three words that rocked his world. That he and Naomi had created a child. That she had kept this from him.

You said you didn't want a kid. Said you didn't want to be a father. His own conscience accused him, yet another part of him knew he was right to be angry. Right to feel a measure of grief that Naomi hadn't told him.

He thought they had been coming to a good place. Now this? She didn't tell him because, in spite of all her talk, she didn't think he'd make a good father either.

He had dared to believe her. Dared to test the idea of their being together.

And now?

She hadn't trusted him then. Didn't trust him now. If she had, she would have told him sooner. In spite of her assurances to the contrary, he couldn't help wonder if Naomi would have kept the secret longer if Allison hadn't forced her hand.

Only Billy had known about his child.

Jess slowed down at the highway, then stomped on the accelerator, slammed the truck through the gears and drove and drove and drove.

Naomi walked back to the house, her heart still beating against her ribs. Her heart felt like a cold center in the hollow of her chest.

She wanted to go after Jess and beg his forgiveness, but anything she had to say would be empty words to him. She had to wait and hope that the next time she saw him she could, again, ask his forgiveness.

Her steps faltered as her thoughts tumbled like rocks down a mountain, heavy and out of control.

What if Jess couldn't forgive her? What if he didn't want her back?

Her old insecurities rose and taunted her. *You were never the kind of girl he wanted. He could do so much better.*

She stopped, her hands pressed to her face as hot tears choked her throat. *Please, Lord, make him come back. Let him come back.*

Loneliness rose and caught her in its relentless grip and then she caught herself. She was alone. She had to deal with this on her own.

"Naomi, honey, what's wrong?" Sheila's voice seemed to come from a faraway place, slowly registering through Naomi's sorrow. "Is everything okay?"

Naomi looked up to see Sheila standing in the doorway of the other house.

She couldn't wrap what had just happened in the tiny medium of words. Not yet. So she simply nodded, then turned and walked back to the house.

Once inside, she sat at the kitchen table where, it seemed like years ago, her reaction to Allison's comments had unleashed this storm.

"Where's Jess?" Sheila was asking. "I saw his truck leave. I thought you went with him, then I saw you outside. What happened?"

Naomi massaged her aching temples, her tears hovering just below the surface of her self-control. "We had a fight."

"What? What about? You two looked so happy when you came back a few hours ago."

We were, Naomi thought. Those bright, silvery moments such a contrast to the anger and anguish she had just experienced.

"What could you two possibly fight about?"

Naomi wanted to tell her, but knew this time she had to do things right. Before she told Sheila, she had to tell her sisters. Her nana.

The thought of facing them with what she had done created a convulsion of shame and guilt. She had always been the good girl. The one who always did the right thing.

"It was...personal," was all she could say. She would have to, sometime or another, tell Sheila, as well. After all, it had been her grandchild Naomi had carried for those few months.

"How's Brittany?" she asked, returning her focus to her patient. For now, this was her job.

"She's doing well," Sheila said with a smile. "It looks as though Scott will be involved in her life. He's been making plans."

"I'm so happy for her." Naomi had her own misgivings about the situation, but the reality was this was what needed to happen.

Children need their father.

She knew that from her own personal experience. How often she had wished her father was around, especially when her mother struggled with the care of three young girls. Thank goodness she had Nana and Papa to help her out.

She thought of Jess and his father and her certainty faltered again.

"Did Jess say how long he would be gone?" Sheila was asking. "I was hoping to get to town this evening. A good friend of mine heard I was around and wanted to get together with me."

Naomi's attention snapped back to the present. "Actually, no. He didn't say how long he'd be gone. You could call him on his cell phone and find out."

"I'm surprised he didn't tell you." Then Sheila held her hand up. "I'm sorry. Of course you wouldn't know. Not if you two were having a fight." Sheila sighed and patted Naomi on her shoulder. "I know you are upset about it, but don't worry, Jess will come around. He was always so crazy about you. I was sad it didn't work out. Of course Jess's father and I were having our own troubles, so we didn't...couldn't be much of a support to him. But he's been happier now than I've seen him in a long time. More settled. More peaceful." Sheila patted her again. "He'll come around. He'll come back."

An hour later the sound of Jess's truck coming up the driveway proved Sheila right.

But half an hour later, without coming to the house he left again. Jess sent a text message to Brittany that she shared with Naomi, saying he needed to get away and would be gone a few days.

Naomi went to bed early that night, pleading a headache. Thankfully Brittany was tired out from the excitement of the day and Sheila left to go visit a friend.

As sleep eluded Naomi, her mind ran over the events of the day. How could a day that had started out with such promise end so badly?

She tried to still her troubled soul. But her mind held an immense, impossibly heavy sadness that she couldn't shift or move no matter how she tried. Jess was gone. And she didn't think he wanted to be with her anymore. Not after what had just happened.

What if she had told Jess right away about the pregnancy? Would he have stood by her? He had been so insistent, so angry when she talked about potential children.

Would he have grieved with her? Or would he have felt the same relief she had seen on Billy's face when she told him about the miscarriage?

The old sorrow of that loss dragged at her, but its fingers weren't as sharp, its pain not as deep as it had been. The heartache had stitched itself into the fabric of her life and had become part of who she was. She couldn't separate it from her identity any more than she could separate her eye color from who she was.

She had come to Rockyview to find out who Naomi Deacon really was. From the time she went back to Billy she felt as if she had lost herself in him.

And now she was in danger of losing herself in Jess. Of thinking he could give her all she needed. When he walked away from her, he took a part of her heart.

But he didn't take her essence with him.

That thought brought her up short.

He didn't take her essence. He didn't take who she truly was.

She was God's child. God knew everything about her and He loved her in spite of that. His grace should be sufficient.

Her heart crumpled at the thought of not having Jess in her life. How could she bear it? She had come so close to a happiness she had only experienced when she was with Jess before only to have it taken away.

Please, Lord, she prayed, *help me to find my identity in You. Only in You. Help me to know that Your love is unconditional and all-forgiving.*

She rolled to her side, hoping to find sleep and as she lay in her bed, in the room that Jess used to sleep in, she sent up a prayer for God to watch over him, as well.

CHAPTER 13

*T*he first thing Jess noticed when he pulled up to his house after being gone for days, was the car. The second thing he noticed was that it wasn't Naomi's car.

Relief was followed by anger, followed by sorrow, which clenched at his heart.

Naomi, who, for as long as he had known her, had been the example of all that was good and true and pure had lied to him. Hadn't trusted him with probably one of the biggest things that had ever happened to him. How do you come back from something like that? She had spent so much time convincing him he was a good person, he started to believe it himself. But in the end she didn't think he needed to know he was going to be a father because she believed the same thing about him. He wouldn't have made a good father.

Jess parked his truck by his house and dropped his head back against the headrest, closing his eyes a minute. His ears still rang from the endless drone of his truck's engine, the only noise he'd heard for the past couple of days.

After Naomi had dropped her bomb on him, he'd had to

leave. He couldn't be around her. He needed to sort out his thoughts and rearrange his emotions. He had come so close to making a really big fool of himself. Last week he had gone to a jeweler to look at engagement rings. That's how close he'd come. He'd been driving for the past three days. He'd gone up over the Rockies into British Columbia. Driven up to Penticton, then the Coquihalla, onto Jasper and down the Columbia Ice Fields Parkway, oblivious to the beauty and majesty of the mountains, only stopping to put gas in the vehicle. He'd driven up the island to Prince Rupert, then taken the ferry back to the mainland, stopping to grab some sleep, something to eat only because he knew he should, then driving some more, trying to outrun the thoughts that plagued him.

Naomi had been expecting his child and hadn't told him. How could she have kept this from him?

You said you didn't want to be a father. What else was she supposed to do?

She could have told him anyway. She could have trusted him.

His anger with her had slowly been replaced by hurt, which had morphed into a kind of numbness.

Okay, Lord, he prayed. *Now what do I do? Where do I go now?*

All his silly plans had to change.

His heart wrenched at the thought. For a few weeks he felt as if his life had shifted in a good direction. He was moving toward a happiness he hadn't felt in years. Not since he had been with Naomi the first time.

Now?

He glanced at the house, wondering if the car belonged to the new nurse Naomi had found for Brittany. He had texted Brittany every day to see how she was doing, so he knew she was fine. He also knew that Naomi had quit and had found someone who was willing to stop by every afternoon and monitor Brittany's health. Brittany didn't want her staying overnight now that Sheila was back, so it worked out.

He should stop by the house, he thought, but he didn't feel like talking to anyone yet. He knew Brittany would ask a hundred questions about Naomi and he was not willing to answer any of them. He had too many himself.

The sound of his booted feet echoed in his empty house, mocking his lonely state, and as he walked up the stairs to his room, again he glanced at the windows where Naomi's stained-glass windows were to go.

Thank goodness she hadn't finished them. They would have been an unwelcome reminder of what he once had and lost again.

He went into his room and dropped onto the bed, then he turned his head sideways and saw his Bible on the bedside table. He picked it up, paging idly through it. He stopped here and there, but nothing spoke to him.

He paged through the Psalms and found a folded-over page, so he turned to it. Psalm 130. At one time something in this Psalm had struck him. So he started reading.

"Out of the depths I cry to You, O Lord; O Lord, hear my voice. Let Your ears be attentive to my cry for mercy."

He felt like he was sending his anger and anguish up into the heavens from the deep, dark place he had descended the past few days.

"If You, O Lord, kept a record of sins, O Lord, who could stand? But with You there is forgiveness."

The words of the Bible passage resonated in his mind, accusing and at the same time oddly reassuring. He knew he wasn't without sin, but it was as if the passage was reminding him that no one could stand in God's presence if God kept a record of wrong.

That included him.

Jess reread the passage, still struggling with all the things that circled in his mind. Naomi. His father.

And behind those thoughts came another one.

Himself.

He had done wrong in so many ways and so often. That Naomi had even been willing to date him in the first place had been a huge surprise. She had been all that was good and wonderful and pure that his hungry soul had been looking for.

And he had ruined it. That there had been consequences to that act had been as much his fault as anyone's. His own conscience accused him. He knew he had been wrong to be angry with her.

And yet...

The errant doubt lingered and he returned to the Bible.

"Oh, Israel, put your hope in the Lord, for with the Lord is unfailing love and with Him is full redemption."

Unfailing love and full redemption.

Strong language that clearly laid things out with no wiggle room. God's love for him was unfailing and His forgiveness complete.

He closed the Bible and closed his eyes. *"Help me, Lord, to forgive. Help me to know that I am as guilty as anyone else."*

He thought of his father and his grandfather. He wanted to hold back forgiveness from them, but then thought of what Naomi had said.

As long as he held back forgiveness, his father had a hold over him. He remembered Naomi saying that forgiveness would free him from bitterness and anger.

If it would free him from his father, maybe it would also free him from Naomi. Except, deep in his heart, he knew he didn't want to be free of her. At all.

Help me do this, Lord, he prayed. *I can't do it on my own.*

"When do you have to go to work?"

Naomi glanced at the clock in the living room of Nana Bond's house. "Not for another half an hour."

Nana sat back in her chair with a faint smile. "I'm glad you finally got a job at the hospital, even if it is only part-time."

"It's a start." After Jess left, Naomi knew she couldn't keep working with Brittany, so she phoned around, praying she would find someone, anyone, to take care of the girl. Thankfully, through Shannon's contacts, she found a retired nurse who was willing to come the next day. As if in answer to prayer, two days after that she got a job at the hospital. She had started last night. Today was the first time she'd had a chance to visit with Nana.

"So what else have you been doing? I thought for sure you'd go back to Mug Shots. After all, you can't pay your bills working only part-time."

Naomi couldn't help a faint smile at Nana's advice. "I've been doing some other work for Allison's parents. Some stained-glass windows for a house Allison's father is building."

Nana frowned. "Stained glass? Is there any money in that? I know you did it before, but nothing came of it."

"There can be." Her thoughts shifted to the windows she had started for Jess. She wondered what he would do with them. "I just have to make a commitment to it."

Nana nodded, but Naomi could see she wasn't convinced.

"So what made you decide to stop working for Jess?" Nana asked her. "I got the impression the two of you were getting back together again."

Pain and guilt bloomed again inside her. "Something happened," Naomi said, the words a lame shadow of the storm of emotions her confession to Jess had caused.

Nana reached over and took Naomi's hand, covering it with hers. "Something?" she prompted.

Naomi looked over at Nana, remembering all the times she,

Hailey, and Shannon would be brought to the ranch by their mother when she couldn't cope anymore.

Nana and Papa Bond were a shelter in the storm of their life. Nana had probably spent more time with her than her own mother had. And Nana could always tell when Naomi wasn't being completely forthright with her.

Naomi looked at her nana and felt a sob rise. She knew she had to tell her the same thing she told Jess. She had suppressed the truth too long.

"Remember how when I came to you all those years ago and told you Jess broke up with me?" Naomi said, fingering her grandmother's worn wedding band.

"Yes, I remember how upset you were. I remember that Hailey wanted to go and beat him up. I also remember how thankful I was you got together with Billy again. I didn't think Jess was the right person for you. He was too, well, wild. Uncontrolled. He didn't seem to have good parents."

"He didn't. That's why he was so wild and uncontrolled. They didn't take good care of him. Especially not his father." She stopped herself, tamping down her anger with the man. What happened to Jess wasn't her story to tell. "Anyway, it didn't go the way I said. Jess and I broke up because we had a fight, that much was true, but there was more going on." She tried to hold Nana's loving gaze but couldn't.

How often had she heard Nana tell Hailey that she should be more like Naomi? How often had she overheard her nana tell people what a good, Christian girl her granddaughter was? How proud Nana was of her?

What would she think now?

She tried to withdraw her hand, but her grandmother wouldn't let her. "Jess and I...we spent a lot of time together. His parents left for a couple of weeks and we were in the house together. Alone. We got intimate." She stopped there, hoping Nana would understand without her having to say the words.

"Oh. Oh, honey."

"I was too ashamed to tell you," Naomi rushed on, hoping to forestall any questions. "I was scared and nervous and didn't know what to do. Jess and I talked about what we did and we both said it wouldn't happen again. We talked about maybe getting married and I was so happy. Then, about six weeks later I found out that I was pregnant."

Her grandmother's swift intake of breath was like a body blow. But she didn't let go of Naomi's hand and Naomi kept talking, knowing she had to get this out.

"I didn't know how to talk to Jess, but I knew I had to tell him. So we talked about what we were doing after we both went to college. We talked about where we were going and I asked about kids. He said absolutely no kids. No way. He was so vehement about that. I knew Jess well enough that he wasn't giving in, but I had to make him try. I was carrying his baby. So I pushed and he pushed back and we had a terrible fight. But I still didn't tell him. I couldn't after all that. After his declaration that he never wanted kids. Then Billy returned and told me he had made a terrible mistake, and that he wanted me back. I thought here was my chance. So I went back, and I told him about the baby. He was disappointed, but at the same time he said he would support me. Then I lost the baby. I saw losing the baby as a final break in my relationship with Jess. Almost like a judgment."

Nana squeezed Naomi's hand even more tightly. "God doesn't work like that," she said quietly. "You know that God is compassionate and gracious—"

"Slow to anger and abounding in love," Naomi continued, automatically finishing the sentence from the Psalm Nana and Papa had gotten her to memorize.

"He does not treat us as our sins deserve nor repay us according to our iniquities. You know He has removed our sins from us as far as the east is from the west. So take those words and take them to heart," Nana said quietly. "You've had a lot to deal with the past while. Losing Billy must have been hard."

Naomi looked up at her grandmother, her sorrow almost choking her. "I never told Jess about the baby until a few days ago. I kept it a secret from him all this time. But as we got closer I knew I had to tell him. And now he doesn't want me in his life, and losing him has been far harder than losing a man I was engaged to for four years. I never loved Billy as much as I love Jess. I miss him and I don't know what to do." Her last words came out on a choked sob and she finally gave in to the tears that had been threatening so long, laid her head on Nana's lap and cried.

Nana simply let her cry, stroking her head, murmuring incoherent endearments. Naomi cried for her lost baby, cried for her lost love, cried for the missed opportunities. And then, when her tears were spent, she lay a moment longer, letting her nana's comfort ease away the pain that clenched her heart every moment of every day since Jess drove away from her.

"I think you need to give Jess some time," her nana was saying, still stroking her hair away from her damp cheeks. "This is a big thing for him to face."

"But you should have seen him when I told him. It was like I punched him in the stomach. Then he looked as if I had betrayed him in the worst possible way. He'll never forgive me."

"Never is a long time," Nana was saying. "And in spite of my misgivings about Jess, I think you two are meant for each other. I think he knows it, too."

Naomi lifted her head, puzzled at Nana's statement. "What do you mean, we're right for each other? You said you didn't want me to date him in the first place."

"He's changed a lot, but it's more than that. I remember seeing you two together at Mug Shots all those years ago. I remember how your face shone. How bright your eyes were. And it wasn't just you. When I saw you with Jess, I saw a couple who lit up the room with their happiness. You were brighter and more full of life than I had ever seen you before."

Her nana's words were both bitter and sweet. Jess did make her feel fully alive. Then and now.

"I see the same thing...saw the same thing recently. The few times I did see you, mind you," she said with a gently scolding tone.

"I had to stay with Brittany," Naomi said. "She needed me there full-time."

"Of course." Nana stroked Naomi's cheek, then tucked her hair back behind her ears.

"So what do I do?"

"For now, nothing except to lay it all at God's feet. He's your loving Father and He knows your heart. He knows Jess's heart, as well. You need to let go. You need to forgive yourself and you need to let Jess find the time to forgive you, too."

"What if he doesn't?"

Nana gave her a melancholy smile. "Then he's not the right person for you, is he?"

Naomi heard the words and tried not to let them pierce her heart. But at the same time, she knew Nana was right.

So, just as she used to as a young girl, she folded her hands in Nana's lap and let her grandmother cover them with hers. Then they both bowed their heads and put Naomi's burden on the shoulders of the one who promised to carry it all.

Naomi knocked lightly on the door to Brittany's hospital room. She knew exactly when Brittany came in to have her baby today. She also knew Jess had been there for the birth, then had left the hospital. Even though she had promised her sister Hailey they were going shopping after work, she knew she couldn't leave the hospital without seeing Brittany while Jess wasn't around.

"Come in," Naomi heard, then stepped into the room.

She walked past the first bed, which was empty, then to the curtained-off area where Brittany lay. Naomi smiled at Sheila who sat on a chair beside the bed, holding a tiny bundle. The baby boy that Brittany had delivered safely only a couple of hours ago.

Brittany looked up, a huge smile on her face. "I was hoping you would come," she said, holding her arms out.

Naomi walked to her side and enveloped her in a tight hug. Then she drew back, noticing a peace on Brittany's face that she hadn't seen before.

"Congratulations. You did good. You certainly don't look like you just had a baby."

"I feel fantastic."

"How is the little guy?" Naomi asked, glancing at Sheila, who was still looking down at the bundle she held.

"He's so beautiful. Do you want to hold him?" Brittany turned to her mother. "Sheila, can Naomi hold Kevin?"

Sheila dragged her attention away from the baby and gave Naomi a broad smile. "Yes, of course."

"It's okay," Naomi said, surprised at the gentle love shining from Sheila's face. She didn't want to take the baby away from the woman who seemed so obviously besotted with the child.

Then Brittany's phone chirped and she gave Naomi an apologetic smile as she covered the phone. "It's Scott," she said. "He's on his way. The baby came sooner than he expected."

"We'll sit over here," Sheila said. "Give you two some privacy."

She got up and moved to the other side of the curtain, still holding the baby.

Naomi walked over to her to get a closer look.

"I don't mind to give him up," Sheila said.

CAROLYNE AARSEN

"That's okay," Naomi murmured, looking down at the tiny head swaddled in the blanket, her heart contracting at the sight. So small and so perfect.

"Please," Sheila said, "you had much more to do with his safe delivery than I did."

Naomi curbed her reluctance, then took the little bundle from Sheila, looking down at the tiny head with its downy fuzz. His eyes were still swollen and red from the trauma of birth. But his mouth was like a tiny bud, pursed and perfect.

Her heart skipped at the sight.

"It's all here," Naomi said reverently, touching his cheek and folding back the blanket enough to touch the tiny fingers with their fingernails smaller than a kernel of rice. "He's so complete and so perfect."

For a fleeting moment she wondered what her and Jess's baby would have looked like. She pressed her lips together against the old sorrow and then, once again, forgave herself.

"He's so precious," she breathed, inhaling that faintly spicy and transitory smell of a newborn baby.

Sheila hovered, her hand resting on the baby's body. "I can't believe he's here already. I thought it would be another month. Thankfully he didn't need to be in the incubator."

"He's a little miracle," Naomi said, glancing Sheila's way, surprised at this woman's reaction.

"He is." Sheila was quiet, her expression suddenly serious. "I can't believe what I feel for this baby. I mean, Brittany isn't even my own daughter, but I can't get enough of this child."

Naomi tried not to feel a beat of resentment at what Sheila was saying. "Did you feel the same way about Jess?" she couldn't help asking.

Sheila's face twisted and Naomi instantly regretted what she said. She had no right to judge Sheila. No right at all.

"I'm sorry," she said quietly. "That was wrong of me. Please forgive me.

Sheila released a bitter laugh. "I'm the one who should be asking forgiveness. From Jess."

"It's not too late," Naomi said.

"And what about you and Jess? What happened?"

"Knock, knock," Hailey's voice whispered from the doorway, breaking the moment and releasing Naomi from the need to say anything.

Hailey grinned when she saw Naomi holding the baby and hurried over. "Is that him? Can I see?" She bent over the tiny bundle Naomi held. "Oh, my goodness, look at that little guy. He's so adorable."

They all stood a moment, three women united in their admiration of this tiny miracle of life. Then Brittany called for Sheila and excusing herself, Sheila left, leaving Naomi still holding Kevin.

"Is Brittany feeling okay?" Hailey asked.

"As far as I know. I haven't talked to anyone yet, but usually once the baby is born, the diabetes eases off," Naomi murmured, stroking the tiny cheek.

"Looks good on you," Hailey said quietly. Then she sighed, slipping her arm around Naomi's shoulder. "I still feel so bad about what happened to you. I wish you would have told us about everything."

"I know I should have, but I was scared," she admitted. "I should have trusted you."

"So how are you doing now?"

"I'm okay. I've carried this for a lot longer than you have."

Hailey lifted Naomi's chin. "You don't look okay. You look sad and weary and even more worn out than after Billy died."

"Probably because I feel worse than I did after Billy died." As soon as the words spilled out she wished she could take them back. Hailey would jump on them, that much she knew for certain.

"I told Jess that he had to be careful with you," Hailey said, her voice growing hard. "I warned him you weren't in a good place. I should have known he wouldn't listen."

"What are you talking about?" Naomi said.

"I talked to Jess a while back. I had my reservations about him, so I told him he had to be careful with you. I remember saying something about him not playing with your emotions. Jess is, well, a bit rough around the edges and I was looking out for you. You are a gentle soul and I was afraid he would take advantage of you again. Emotionally, I mean."

Naomi released a bitter laugh. "Thanks, I think, but you didn't need to stand up for me. Especially not with Jess."

"What are you talking about? You were devastated after he broke up with you the first time and you're not looking too great right now either. He's not good for you."

Naomi looked down at the baby she held, this completely innocent child, and wondered about Jess's childhood. Wondered what it had been like for him living with a father he was afraid of and a mother who didn't stand up for him.

"Jess is the best person I know," she said quietly. "His actions speak louder than his words, and his actions are the ones of a sincere, caring man. You say he broke my heart?" She released a bitter laugh. "I think I broke his, too. I should have trusted him, but I didn't give him the chance. I should have stayed instead of running back to Billy when he crooked his finger in my direction." She looked over at Hailey, hoping her sister understood. "Billy took me back in spite of me carrying Jess's child, but he never let me forget what he did. Jess took in Brittany who is no relation to him. A girl who was sixteen and pregnant. But I never, not once, heard him say anything to her that made her feel like she was less of a person. He never judged her." Naomi looked down at the nugget hanging from around her neck, thinking of August Bond and the choice he made, then looked back at her sister, trying to keep her emotions under control. "I should have chosen Jess. I should have made a decision to stay with him. I took the easy way out and ran away. I left him and I didn't even do him the justice of letting him know I was carrying his baby. It was a huge mistake and I hope that someday he can forgive me for that. I don't deserve it, but I am hoping he will. Because I still care for him. More than I've ever cared for anyone else. He's the best person I know and I don't deserve him."

She looked away from Hailey, then down at Kevin wondering if the pounding of her heart would frighten him.

Hailey didn't say anything and Naomi was thankful for the momentary reprieve.

Then she caught the movement of a body in the doorway. Scott was here, she thought. Then the body moved from the shadow into the light of the room and her heart dropped into her stomach.

It was Jess.

CHAPTER 14

$\mathcal{H}$e couldn't breathe.

All he could do was stare at Naomi, wondering if he heard correctly. Wondering if she meant what she had just said.

"Hey, Jess," Hailey said in a falsely jovial voice. "How long have you been here?"

"Long enough."

He couldn't look away from Naomi who was staring at him, remnants of surprise and shock still showing on her face. She swallowed, then looked down at Kevin, pulling in a long, wavery breath.

"I'm sorry..." Her voice faltered and she pressed her lips together.

"Why don't I take that baby," Hailey said, gently removing Kevin from Naomi's arms. "And maybe you and Jess can go for a walk or something?"

Naomi easily relinquished the tiny form and Jess saw how her gaze lingered on Kevin. Was she thinking of the baby she lost?

He took a step closer to her. "Naomi..."

She shook her head, still looking down. "I'm so sorry, Jess. I'm so sorry."

Her apology wrung at his heart and he swallowed down a peculiar knot of sorrow.

"I think Hailey had a good suggestion," he said quietly. "Do you want to come with me?" He held out his hand.

She looked at it, then slowly held out her own and placed it in his. He squeezed, then gave her a gentle tug and she followed him.

They walked down the hall, saying nothing, then out the door and down the street. They were both quiet, as if readying themselves for whatever might come.

Finally he came to the baseball diamonds and he stopped there, sitting down on the worn wooden bleachers. Naomi sat down beside him, still clinging to his hand.

Finally she turned to him.

"I was wrong. I know that. I wanted to tell you, but I didn't know when to do it."

Jess held her gaze, then reached up and gently pressed his finger to her nose. "I'm sorry, too. There's been a lot of misunderstanding between us." He let his fingers linger on Naomi's face. "But I understand now. At least a bit better. When I first saw Brittany with that baby I realized you weren't a whole lot older than she was when you found out you were pregnant. Of course you'd be scared."

She reached up and took his hand, folding hers around it, reinforcing the connection. "I was afraid," she said quietly. "When you said you couldn't be a father, I got scared that you would reject me if I told you about the baby. I was scared and I was alone. I'd always been the good girl. The one who never did anything wrong and then this. Then Billy...he asked me to come back to him. I told him about the baby and he said he would take me back."

Jess let his fingers caress her cheek, feeling her pain and loneliness. "I'm sorry, too."

Then he bent over and brushed a kiss over her mouth. "But I'm not sorry I heard what I did a few minutes ago."

She held his gaze, her own earnest. "I meant every word. You're a good man. I've always thought that and I've always loved you." She held his gaze, a melancholy smile slipping over her features. "You were my everything. Even when I was with Billy."

She was quiet and Jess knew enough to allow her this moment.

"Then I came back here and it was as if all those turbulent emotions and all our history threatened to take over. And it scared me. I needed to know who I was. I needed to find out who I am." She looked over at him. "I feel like so much of my life has been spent living in the shadow of my sisters and then in the shadow of you. Even what I had with Billy was like the shadow of a relationship—an eternal engagement and no wedding in sight. Then he died. And I came back to Rockyview and there you were. Even more appealing and handsome than when I dated you. And I got scared again. I wanted to stay away from you. I wanted space from you and from the guilt I felt whenever I saw you. I was afraid that if I let myself, I would get pulled back into that swirl of emotions that was our relationship and I would lose myself in the shadows of the past again."

"Is that how you see it? Losing yourself?"

"I feel as if most of my life I haven't known who I am."

"I always knew who you were. I always knew about you."

"No, you didn't!" She released a light laugh. "You were the most popular guy in school. The guy every girl wanted to date. I was just Naomi."

"You were never just Naomi to me."

"Really?" Her incredulity surprised him. He had always

thought of her as more confident. "I was nobody. A girl people didn't remember."

He moved closer, determined to make her realize just how much a part of his life she had been.

"In grade eight you got a pair of red boots," he said, holding her gaze, determined to let her know. "You wore them every day for a month. In grade nine, you got a black eye from running into the volleyball net during a practice I was watching. You used to come to the ski hill with Hailey and you always wore a purple coat and red ski pants I figured you had bought at the New to You store in town. You cut your hair short in grade ten and I hated it, and when you grew it out, I was glad. In grade eleven you used to sit in the cafeteria with a book and a set of headphones and I remember thinking that maybe you did that because you broke up with Billy and I had a moment of hope, but I found out he was doing track that year and was busy. I didn't know what was going on in grade twelve because by that time I was supposed to be done. Then you broke up with Billy and you came and tutored me. And then my life took the best turn it ever did. And here I am, as crazy about you now as I was then. Probably more."

Naomi's eyes widened as he listed his litany of how important she had been in his life. And right now he didn't care. Because right now he needed her to know she had always been a part of his past and, Lord willing, would be a part of his future.

She blinked, as if trying to understand. "I can't... I don't..."

He resisted the urge to kiss her and instead said, "When you left, it was like there was a hole in my life that only you could fill. You never stood in the shadows with me. You were always a bright light in my life. Someone whose life I wanted to be a part of. Someone who I need in my life."

There it was. The declaration that he'd tried to hold back but finally couldn't.

"I love you, Naomi Deacon. I know we've had some missteps, but I also know that God's love covers a lot. That He removes our sins from us."

"As far as the east is from the west," Naomi said with a note of wonder in her voice.

"And probably farther." He eased out a sigh. "I know I have a lot of stuff going on in my life and I'm still struggling to forgive my father, but you were right about that. I have to if I'm going to be free from him. But I also know with you at my side, it will be a lot easier. You're a bright light in my life and with you, I feel complete. Whole. I don't want us to be apart anymore. I want us to be together. I want you to be my wife. To move into that house with me. To have children with me." His voice broke a little on that last sentence, but he didn't care.

Naomi reached up and cradled his face, a glimmer of tears in her eyes. "I want that, too. More than anything." Then she leaned forward and pressed a kiss to his lips. "I love you, Jess. I don't think I ever stopped loving you."

He drew her close to him, kissed her again and again, then tucked her head in the hollow between his shoulder and his neck. "Don't ever stop. I don't want us ever to be apart again."

"Neither do I."

He kissed her again, then drew back. "I suppose we should go back."

Naomi nodded. "Though I suspect Hailey, Brittany, and your mother have a good idea what's going on."

"So we may as well let them know." He got up, caught her by the hand and drew her to her feet. He felt a curious reluctance, but at the same time a desire to shout out to anyone who wanted to know.

Naomi and him.

Together again. Just the way it should be.

If you want to spend even more time in Rockyview, I've got another series coming up - Family Promises.

The first book in that series is Ever Caring.

Here's a sample to whet your appetite:

EVER CARING

Just go in. It's just an office. A building.

Renee stood just outside the door of Arlan Truscott, Barrister and Solicitor, surprised that the pounding of her heart wasn't echoing in the entrance.

The last time she'd been here, she'd sat in Arlan's office and signed papers that haunted her still.

That was ten long years ago.

With a decisive nod and a quick sucking in of her breath, she pushed the door open and entered the office.

The woman sitting behind the wooden desk dominating the reception area looked up, a headset nested in her teased blond hair, and smiled. "Hey, Renee, you're early."

"I hope that's okay?" Renee asked, her eyes flicking over the interior of the office, noting the changes.

Now the walls were painted a soft, colonial blue instead of the puce-green imprinted on her memory. A colour that could still make her nauseous. She clutched the handle of her shoulder bag and suppressed the dark thoughts, turning back to Debbie. "Is Mr. Truscott ready to see me?"

"There's been a change in plans. Mr. Truscott was called away, but his son, Zach, will take over your file."

That was puzzling, but she was secretly relieved. Though Rockyview wasn't large, she still ran into Mr. Truscott from time to time. Though it got easier, once in awhile the memories would assault her but over time she had learned to smooth off the rough edges. However, sheer necessity had forced her to set up an appointment with him today.

"Have you met Zach?" Debbie asked.

"No. Not yet," Renee said. "Though I have heard about him."

Then the door of the other office opened, and Renee got to her feet to meet Zach Truscott herself.

He looked to be in his mid-thirties, tall, slender, thick blond hair waving away from a strong-featured face. His blue eyes flicked from the file he held to her, and when he smiled, she couldn't stop an answering lift of her heart.

Classically handsome, she thought, yet with eyes that seemed to hold a shadow of sadness. Through her friend Evangeline, Renee had heard that Zach Truscott was a widower, that he had a young daughter and that he'd moved to Rockyview from Toronto two weeks ago to help his father with his growing legal business. Evangeline knew all this because Zach boarded his horses at her father's ranch.

"Good morning, Ms. Albertson," Zach said, holding his hand out to take hers. "I'm Zach Truscott. I'm sorry my father couldn't see you this morning. He had some unexpected business to take care of."

Renee took his hand, his firm grip creating the faintest tingle in her palm.

She shook her feelings aside, attributing them as a normal reaction to an attractive male. She was still single, after all, as her mother frequently pointed out to her.

As if she had any time for men. She had a disabled mother to take care of and a business to sell. And it was the latter that brought her here today.

"My father gave me your file this morning," Zach said, standing aside to let her precede him into his office. He walked around the desk and dropped into the chair across from her. "He said you're in the process of selling your business?"

Renee nodded, settling into the straight-backed wooden chair across from him. As she did, she darted a quick glance around the room, stifling the chills that chased each other down her spine as memories intruded. This was a different time. Different lawyer. Different office.

The walls in here were painted a cheerful yellow. A large bookcase covered one wall with the usual assortment of legal books. To one side, however, she saw a small red table and chair covered with papers and crayons and paints. A pink electronic device sat on one corner of the table emitting glowing green light. On the wall above that table was an assortment of framed pictures. One of them was of a stunningly beautiful woman. She held the hand of a little girl with tousled blond hair and a gap-toothed smile. They were backlit by a large window that overlooked the city of Toronto.

Taken from the CN Tower, Renee assumed, her heart turning over at the sight of the little girl.

"That's my daughter," Zach said, catching the direction of Renee's curious gaze. "Addison. She's eight."

"She's adorable," Renee said past the sudden thickness in her throat. Why did this happen to her every time she saw a girl of that age?

Please, Lord, help me concentrate. Help me let go. That was in the past. I've moved on.

Her prayer eased her heartbeat back to normal, then she looked back at Zach. "How does she like living in Rockyview?" she asked, determined to have an ordinary conversation. "I imagine it's quite a change from Toronto."

"She loves it. Especially because we have a place to keep our horses that's closer than where we boarded them in Ontario."

"So you and your daughter ride?"

"Not as often as we'd like, but I'm hoping that will change once we're settled in. Addison and I are still trying to find a rhythm here, and I'm trying not to worry about her all the time. Hard to break old habits," he said.

She caught an edge of tension in his voice and wondered once again about his situation. Rumor had it that his wife had died almost a year ago. That was why he'd moved back to Rockyview.

"But enough about that." Zach flipped open the manila folder and pulled out a piece of paper, obviously getting back to business.

She couldn't help a niggling regret. Zach seemed easy to talk to, and she had enjoyed the ordinary conversation they had shared, even for a moment. It had been a while since she'd had a normal interaction with a man. Any guy she had dated since her mother's accident had had to deal with the reality that Renee's mother and her disabilities was a priority for her. None of them could.

"So you want to sell your business?" Zach was saying, his voice anchoring her back to the present.

Renee nodded. "Yes, the buyer, Cathy, is eager to get the final paperwork done and so am I. I'm assuming that's why your father called me here?"

Zach sat back in his chair. He wore a white button-down shirt with a tie, but the tie was loosened, and the cuffs of the sleeves were rolled up. He looked casually disheveled yet had an air of command, which felt oddly reassuring.

"Unfortunately, we can't sign off on the sale just yet."

Renee felt cold bloom in her chest. "Why not?" Things had to get moving. Her mother's appointments to see the therapist were scheduled. They needed the money from this sale before the treatment began, and she didn't want Ned and Cathy, the buyers, to change their minds. Her kind of business was niche and required someone with a measure of expertise.

"There's been a builder's lien filed against the property about three days ago."

"What? By whom? The renovations on the store were finished two months ago." Fixing up the back rooms of the store had cost her more than she had budgeted for, but it had been a condition of the sale, which had been delayed a couple of times already. "I paid Benny Alpern in full for his work."

"Benny was the general contractor?" Zach asked, glancing down at the file again.

"That's correct," Renee said, trying not to let panic overwhelm her as she leaned forward. She'd had a hard enough time just coming to this office—now things wouldn't be finalized today? And, worse, the sale would be put off? What would happen to her mother? The clock was ticking, and she was running out of time.

Want to read more?

Order Ever Caring by visiting Amazon and search for Every Caring by Carolyne Aarsen

As well, if you enjoyed reading Finding Home, it would be awesome, amazing, tremendous, stupendous and heart-warming if you could leave a review. Reviews help other readers discover my books and help other readers share in the adventures awaiting them in Rockyview. And it's a place worth visiting!

Thanks bunches and take care.

Carolyne

OTHER SERIES

FAMILY BONDS

#1 SEEKING HOME

A rancher who suffered a tragic loss. A single mother on the edge. Can these two find the courage to face a romantic new beginning?

#2 CHOOSING HOME

If you like emergency room drama, second chances, and quaint small-town settings, then you'll adore this romance.

#3 COMING HOME

He thought she chose a hotel over him. She thought he loved money more than her. Years later, can they fill the emptiness in their hearts?

#4 FINDING HOME

She's hiding a terrible truth. He's trying to overcome his scandalous history. Together, forgiveness might give them a second chance.

FAMILY TIES

Four siblings trying to finding their way back to family and faith

A COWBOY'S REUNION

He's still reeling from the breakup. She's ashamed of what she did. Can a chance reunion mend the fence, or are some hearts forever broken? If you like second chance stories, buried passions, and big country settings, then you'll love this emotional novel.

"I enjoyed this book and had trouble putting it down and had to finish it. If the rest of this series is this great, I look forward to reading more books by Carolyne Aarsen." Karen Semones - Amazon Review

THE COWBOY'S FAMILY

She's desperate. He's loyal. Will a dark lie hold them back from finding love on the ranch? If you like determined heroines, charming cowboys, and family dramas, then you'll love this heartfelt novel.

"What a wonderful series! The first book is Cowboy's Reunion. Tricia's story begins in that book. Emotional stories with wonderful characters. Looking forward to the rest of the books in this series." Jutzie - Amazon reviewer

TAMING THE COWBOY

A saddle bronc trying to prove himself worthy to a father who never loved him. A wedding planner whose ex-fiancee was too busy chasing his own dreams to think of hers. Two people, completely wrong for each other who yet need each other in ways they never realized. Can they let go of their own plans to find a way to heal together?

"This is the third book in the series and I have loved them all. . . . can't wait to see what happens with the last sibling." - Amazon reviewer

THE COWBOY'S RETURN

The final book in the Family Ties Series:

He enlisted in the military, leaving his one true love behind.

She gave herself to a lesser man and paid a terrible price.

In their hometown of Rockyview, they can choose to come together or say a final goodbye...

"This author did an amazing job of turning heartache into happiness with realism and inspirational feeling." Marlene - Amazon Reviewer

SWEETHEARTS OF SWEET CREEK

Come back to faith and love

#1 HOMECOMING

Be swept away by this sweet romance of a woman's search for belonging and second chances and the rugged rancher who helps her heal.

#2 - HER HEARTS PROMISE

When the man she once loved reveals a hidden truth about the past, Nadine has to choose between justice and love.

#3 - CLOSE TO HIS HEART

Can love triumph over tragedy?

#4 - DIVIDED HEARTS

To embrace a second chance at love, they'll need to discover the truths of the past and the possibilities of the future...

#5 - A HERO AT HEART

If you like rekindled chemistry, family drama, and small, beautiful towns, then you'll love this story of heart and heroism.

#6 - A MOTHER'S HEART

If you like matchmaking daughters, heartfelt stories of mending broken homes, and fixer-upper romance, then this story of second chances is just right for you.

HOLMES CROSSING SERIES

The Only Best Place is the first book in the Holmes Crossing Series.

#1 THE ONLY BEST PLACE

One mistake jeopardized their relationship. Will surrendering her dreams to save their marriage destroy her?

#2 ALL IN ONE PLACE

She has sass, spunk and a haunting secret.

#3 THIS PLACE

Her secret could destroy their second chance at love

#4 A SILENCE IN THE HEART

Can a little boy, an injured kitten and a concerned vet with his own past pain, break down the walls of Tracy's heart?

#5 ANY MAN OF MINE

Living with three brothers has made Danielle tired of guys and cowboys. She wants a man. But is she making the right choice?

#6 A PLACE IN HER HEART

Her new boss shattered her dreams and now she has to work with him. But his vision for the magazine she loves puts them at odds. Can they find a way to work together or will his past bitterness blind him to future love.

Made in the USA
Monee, IL
15 January 2023

25342443R20121